THE HOLLOW

Samara Risner

The Hollow

ISBN: 978-1-7378974-4-6 *(paperback)*
ISBN: 978-1-7378974-5-3 *(eBook)*

Edited by: *Andrea Grow (my beautiful mother)*
Book cover design by: *Nabin Karna*
Formatted by: *Accuracy4sure*

Contact the author my email <u>samara__06@hotmail.com</u> (two _)
Or join her on her YouTube channel
Mom Of Many

A note to the reader: Child Trafficking is a very hard subject to write and to read. There are some traumatic instances in this book to be aware of. I do my best as an author to handle these situations with grace and to keep things behind closed doors. My hope is that this book urges readers to pray for what is happening all around us. To bring Child Trafficking to the One who can truly make a difference, that He may soften the hearts of the heartless.

The Hollow is a book of fiction. The locations, characters and incidents are all from the author's imagination and are not to be thought of as real events. Any resemblance to a person or event is coincidental.

Other Books by the author:

The Underground Series

The Imaginarium

The Residence

The Hollow

Dedication

This series is dedicated to my girls, Lilah Rayne, Loralye Jane and Lailey Elaine. My love for you is unconditional and unwavering. Continue to strive after Jesus with all that you have, no matter what your circumstances are. He is ALWAYS with you, and so is my mama heart.

Chapter One

North Carolina, November 22nd, 1963

Loralye Wallace pulled her hands out of the soapy dish water and dried them on the floral towel that draped the counter to her right. She looked over at the clock, 6:50 in the morning. With just enough time to have one more cup of coffee with her husband Abe before work, she poured herself a steaming cup before sitting opposite him at the kitchen table.

"Thank you for breakfast Loralye, I'm looking forward to taking you to dinner tonight. Just think of it, no nighttime dishes." He put his paper down, giving her his undivided attention.

"Where should we go? Bubba Ray's? Catherine's Place?"

She smiled at him as she sipped her coffee. Friday nights were her favorite. Date night! Abe insisted that they keep the weekly ritual even though it hurt their very modest budget.

"Why don't we go down by the shore and try one of those places by the beach? I heard that they have some of the best fish in town." She said, the thought of the warm crispy fish making her stomach turn in anticipation.

"Sounds great. You know I can't say no to some fish fried right. I'll come home and pick you up at five."

He finished his coffee, scooted his chair back, and walked around to kiss her on the cheek. Kneeling, he put one of his dark hands on her swelling belly, his long fingers almost spanning her

1

entire bump. He said, "Little man, you keep your mama safe today you hear?"

Getting up, he grabbed his cup and placed it in the water Loralye had left at the bottom of the sink. With one hand on the back door, Loralye stopped him with her no-nonsense tone.

"Abe if you keep calling this child a boy and it comes out a girl, I have a feeling you're going to be mighty disappointed."

He smiled his bright white smile and said, "I told you, it's a boy. I just know it."

He ducked his head under the door frame and headed to work. Loralye smiled, got up, and washed their two coffee mugs before heading to her job which was only a few blocks away.

She enjoyed the scenery as she slowly took her time walking to her cleaning job at the Kreese's home. With her ever-growing belly making it too hard to continue her full-time job across town at a local hotel, she had put in her notice at the insistence of her overprotective husband who wanted her to take it easy. Not ready to just sit at home and twiddle her thumbs for two more months, they had compromised on a two-hour-a-day job for a wealthy family they knew from church.

Cooking, cleaning, and playing with Mrs. Kreese's young twin boys brought excitement at what the future was going to bring for her and Abe. She envisioned their baby a few years from now and prayed a silent prayer that this little blessing she was carrying would indeed be a boy, just like her Abe wanted.

"Just don't come out as big as him," she chuckled to herself.

One of the concessions of her part-time job was that she would be walking to work. She wanted to stay in as good a shape as possible. Loralye was going to do everything in her power to have a decent delivery when the time came.

Walking up the steps to the beautiful two-story colonial-style home, she knocked on the door. Elizabeth Kreese answered almost as soon as Loralye finished knocking and began speaking immediately in her thick southern drawl.

"Loralye, how many times must I tell you to just come on in here? We are as close as family, you and me. I despise that you come here to clean and not just chat away with me instead. Lord knows my husband would appreciate my tongue getting a little exercise before he comes home, so he doesn't have to listen to the training for my verbal marathon that I somehow cannot stop preparing for."

She stepped aside and made way for Loralye to enter.

"You and I both know that I couldn't stand to sit still and do nothing, Mrs. Kreese. This here arrangement has been a blessing more than you will ever know."

Elizabeth waved her hands in dismissal before continuing her verbal word-spewing.

"Oh, I wish you would call me Elizabeth. You and I are closer than last names Loralye."

She smiled gingerly, warmth radiating from her inner kindness that couldn't be ignored by anyone.

Just then, her two boys, John David and Gregory Charles came running in one after the other.

"Slow down you two! Why don't you go outside for a bit? Your energy is about to make me spin in circles."

John David began to laugh at the thought of his proper mother spinning around in the middle of their foyer with company present.

"Mama, you should try it! It's fun spinning until you can't stand no's more."

"No more, you mean. I had my days of spinning long ago. Now, you two scoot on out and I will call you in for a snack here in a bit."

She walked them to the back door and sent them on their next adventure.

Loralye had followed her to the back of the house and wandered into the kitchen. Taking off her Jacket, she got to work in the room that was three times the size of her own. Turning on the hot water, she plugged the sink and added soap to the swirling stream while she straightened up the counter. Beginning on the breakfast dishes, Loralye smiled at the kicks that were coming from her little helper.

Elizabeth came in, poured herself a cup of tea and took a seat at the small table by an oversized window that looked onto the backyard.

"I truly hate to see you washing our dishes being so pregnant. How are you feeling today?" she asked with genuine interest.

"I'm feeling good really, and I don't mind dishes, Mrs. Kreese. It was hard for me to stop working at the hotel, but Abe insisted. You would think I was made of glass, the way he has babied me since I have been expecting. This truly does give me something to keep busy while we wait for this little one to make its way out into the world."

"You are glowing my dear friend. I cannot wait to spoil that little one. It's been four years since I have had the chance to spoil a baby. I still can't believe the twins are almost five. They tell you it goes by quickly, but it doesn't hit you until you have your own flesh and blood growing leaps and bounds every hour."

Elizabeth took a quick breath before she continued to give Loralye a recap of the first few years of John David's and Gregory Charles's lives.

After the kitchen was placed back in order, Elizabeth handed Loralye a small list of things that needed to be done in the next few weeks.

"There is no rush on any of these things. You move so quickly that it's been hard to come up with enough to keep you busy for two hours, five days a week. And truly, please sit and rest whenever you feel the need. All this nonsense can most certainly wait for another time."

Loralye took the missive and read over it. Dust the office, clean the staircase rail, but not the baseboards, (in all capital letters). Change the sheets in the guest room... She was thankful for the tasks she had been given and the generosity of her employer for keeping the harder tasks for another time.

Elizabeth was now outside, and Loralye decided it best to start at the top of the list and work her way down. She still had an hour left and could finish at least the first two things that day. Getting her supplies, she headed into Mr. Kreese's office and began dusting.

Loralye had only been in the office a few times; never had she been asked to dust. Not quite sure where she should begin, she headed to the hundreds of books that lined his shelves and started the monotonous task of dusting each one carefully.

Being a lawyer, he had books that ranged from law school to early church history. She admired his ability to learn, and the desire he had to know more about the church of old. Loralye hadn't spoken with him often, only a few times in passing on Sunday mornings. Sometimes, if she stayed to chat with Elizabeth on days when she didn't have anything going on, she might see him for his lunch briefly, but she wouldn't say she knew him well.

Finishing with the books, she did feel as if she knew him in a new way. It was interesting that you could get a glimpse into someone's head by what they read. The reminder gave her a new want to get into her Bible, the hope that people would glimpse the words she continually hid in her heart, hitting her in a way it never had before.

Walking over to his desk, Loralye began to straighten it up as well. She threw away a few pieces of scrap paper, got an empty glass from beside his leather chair, and then began to sweep up all the dust she had wiped off the books and onto the floor.

A small chest sat under the lone window that looked over the backyard. She wondered if he sat there and watched his handsome boys like Elizabeth had that very morning from the kitchen. She again hoped that Abe would get his boy, knowing he was going to be the best dad in all of North Carolina.

She walked over to the window and watched as Elizabeth spun around in circles, a hand covering her eyes with her two boys sitting cross-legged, giggling while she did her best to stay on two feet. Loralye laughed and hoped she would be just as carefree as a mother.

Stepping away from the window, she noticed that the trunk's lid was slightly open. A white blanket of some sort was peeking from one side of the lid. She looked at the clock. Ten minutes left before her shift ended. She figured that would be enough time to fold the blankets in the trunk before heading back home for the day. Lifting the lid, she peered inside to finish off her shift.

Loralye stepped out back to say goodbye as had become customary.

"Thank you, Mrs. Kreese, I will be back Monday morning."

"You can't stay for a bit today? I wanted to talk to you about baby names! One of the most exciting parts of parenthood is choosing what your children will be known by for the rest of their lives, don't you think?"

Glancing up at Loralye for the first time since she had exited the home, concern worked its way to Elizabeth's soft features.

"Loralye, you look as if you have seen a ghost. Whatever is the matter?"

She walked over to her and grabbed ahold of Loralye's arm to steady her.

Loralye clasped tighter to her bag, pulling her jacket close.

"Nothing at all Mrs. Kreese, I think that I just need a mid-day nap."

"Do you want me to drive you home?"

"Oh, that isn't necessary in the least. A walk will do me some good."

"Well, if you're certain you're okay."

"I am. Thank you, and I will see you Monday."

With that Loralye headed home, walking faster than she ever had before.

Chapter Two

Loralye paced the living room floor, her heart racing faster than it ever had before. She wasn't sure if it was more from her speedy walk home or from what was going on inside her head. What was she going to do? There was no way she could go back to work on Monday. Where was Abe?

She took the few steps to the kitchen to check the clock, it was only 11:30, and she still had hours before Abe would be home. Deciding she needed to distract her mind, she turned on their new radio, dialed through the few channels that were available to her and settled on KLIF 1190 AM radio.

Unable to relax, she sat upright against her pea-green floral sofa. She began tapping her foot rapidly on the floor, her babe kicking consistently along with her. She was listening absent-mindedly to the parade that was going on in Texas. Abe had been talking about John F. Kennedy making an appearance there all week.

The man on the other end of her box radio was talking about all the safety measures that had been put into place, and how the crowd was anticipating John F. Kennedy's arrival all morning. Loralye tried to concentrate on what the broadcaster was saying. She was trying to do anything she could to get her mind off Mr. Kreese and what she had found in his office.

She went to the kitchen and poured herself a glass of milk, deciding that she needed to put her thoughts on the table until Abe could work things out with her. She glanced at the clock, 12:15. She decided to fold their laundry while she listened to the parade.

Everything else was going to have to wait a few hours anyway, so she may as well give it on over to the good Lord to keep ahold of until she could yoke herself with her husband and decide how they were going to move forward.

With new resolve, she took her laundry basket in one hand, putting the pressure of the basket on her hip to help with its weight. Holding a glass of milk in the other, she headed to the living room. Turning up the radio slightly, she enjoyed the excitement of the crowd she could hear behind the man who was detailing everything that was happening moment by moment.

She folded the new baby clothes that she had sewed just the week before. They were all blue. Loralye shook her head, just imagining a little girl coming into the world with nothing to wear that would suit her fragile beauty. For the third time that day, she said a quick prayer to the Lord, just making sure He knew that a boy would be mighty fine.

She took a sip of her milk, imagining the first lady's beauty as the radio host talked about her bright pink suit and black shoes as she exited Air Force One. They handed her a bouquet of red roses, Loralye wondered how she was supposed to carry those around all day. "No one has a sense for nothing," she said aloud, not understanding why they wouldn't wait until they reached the luncheon before handing her the flowers.

The first lady walked behind her husband, the President, as they headed towards the limousine that awaited them.

"The presidential car is now occupied," she heard the man say on the radio, as she folded a pair of tiny booties with care.

The man, who was her only current companion, continued to tell of their exact route, naming the roads they would take. His excitement was tangible through the small speaker, bringing the event right into her home. Loralye finally forgot about what was in the trunk in Mr. Kreese's office and lay on her sofa. Legs up, she allowed herself to relax, milk in hand, with the bottom of the glass resting on her bump.

"The President is now out of his limousine. He is walking, shaking hands. Mrs. Kennedy is shaking hands with the hundreds who came to view their arrival."

Loralye closed her eyes and imagined shaking hands with the first lady in the bright pink suit.

The man talked about how the President loved to make these impromptu stops, meeting the people that he served face to face. Loralye wondered what kind of man would give his life to serve in such a way. She hoped that his heart would always stay as humble as it seemed to be.

She was looking forward to hearing the address that J.F.K. would be making that very day. She wondered if Abe was listening from his work at the garage, and knew he was. Abe talked often of politics and what needed to happen to end segregation, especially in the South.

Thinking of where they lived, bile rose to her throat. The milk that had been resting on her stomach tumbled to the floor as Loralye raced to the bathroom. She barely made it before losing everything in her stomach.

Fear began to grip her heart again. Should they leave this place for good? They had talked about moving somewhere where they were accepted by everyone. Sure, they had their church friends, and Abe had his co-workers, but it was still hard to see separate areas to dine in restaurants, and separate schools for their children.

The Carolinas still had a long way to go before things would be made right if they ever would get to where she hoped they would. She and Abe prayed every night that the hate towards their skin would one day disappear, just as the sharp cool air did when summer came around in full force. She knew it would take the Lord to soften the hearts of the people and she dearly hoped it was in His plan.

Sitting on the cool black and white checkered tile, Loralye prayed that racism would stop before her son would understand what people thought of him. She prayed that he would never feel the embarrassment and pain that came along with the beautiful dark hue of skin that she and Abe bore. She truly would never understand why the color of your skin could decide how someone would treat you.

One of the reasons Loralye was so thankful for Elizabeth Kreese was that she never looked at her skin. She treated her as she was, a woman who worked hard and loved the Lord, just like her. How could such a wonderful lighthearted woman be married to such a horrid man? Loralye put her hands over her eyes and wept for the lost hopelessness of the situation.

What was she going to tell Elizabeth? Was she aware of the hatred in her husband's heart? Was she aware of what was going on in her very home? Loralye couldn't believe it. Elizabeth had to be oblivious to what was going on. There was just no other answer.

After her muscles cried out for the hundredth time, Loralye forced herself to get up off the floor. She rinsed her mouth out with water from the sink before heading back into the living room. She grabbed a washcloth from the kitchen, wetted it down, and went to clean up the literal spilled milk she had cried over.

On her hands and knees reaching under the sofa she said to herself, "Don't you be crying over spilled milk now Loralye Wallace. What would your mother say?" She chuckled at the ever-present saying recited by her mother when she was little.

Loralye listened to the advertisements for formula and headache medicine as she finished folding her laundry. When the man came back on the air, she was shocked to hear him say that the President had been shot.

She sat down, not knowing how her body would handle the shock. Singing came over the radio as another commercial break began. She could care less about what they were selling. She wanted to know what was going on in Texas.

Finally, the man came back on. He said that the President had been shot more than once, his body falling on his wife. "Lord please no." Loralye hoped that he would make it. The Governor of Texas had also been shot. What was their world coming to? So much violence in a place that was begging for peace.

With so much uncertainty and so much internal turmoil, Loralye began to fear for more than just her rights as a woman of color. She feared for her country and what was to come. While on her knees, she placed her wet rag aside and began to pray.

Abe startled her when he came rushing in a few minutes later. He ran to her aid and helped her from the crouching position, lifting her with ease. Her weight was nothing in his strong arms.

"Loralye, we need to get out of this town, now."

The panic behind his words caused the earlier tremors to return.

"As soon as the president was shot, someone threw a brick through the shop window. Clarence said we's best to get out of town until things cool down."

Abe didn't stop talking as he led her to their bedroom to pack. Loralye began to fill her suitcase with their essentials as quickly as she could.

"Abe, are we really in danger?" She paused, holding two of her drop waist style dresses grasped in each hand.

He stopped packing and crossed the room in two large steps. He held her close and stroked her back with one hand, holding her tightly to himself with the other.

"I'm not going to lie to you Loralye, I have been hearing that there is a group of men here in town who don't mean no good to us."

She pressed away from him gently, looking into his eyes and a burning fire of hate came into her being.

"Do you mean the Ku Klux Klan Abe?"

His head fell in defeat as he let the weight of his child's future fall upon his shoulders.

"I think that we need to get out of North Carolina as quickly as we can. We can't take the car either, they are targeting us. I had a note on my car when I left the shop."

He pulled it out of his pocket and handed it to her to read. She couldn't even say the evil words out loud.

"Do you think the Kreese's will help us get over the border? Maybe we could hide out there until nightfall?" he asked her as he continued to pack his bag, grabbing socks out of his top drawer.

Loralye stopped and turned towards him. "I don't think that is an option."

"Why not? Elizabeth would do anything for you. I think it's our best chance of getting out of here in one piece."

Her eyes expelled hot tears as she closed her lids together before whispering, "I pulled a white hooded robe out of Mr. Kreeses' office this very morning."

Chapter Three

———————————

As they continued packing, a loud crash sounded from the living room. Abe jumped across the bedroom, shielding his wife and babe with his oversized body. Loralye warmed at his selflessness; she loved Abe with all her heart. As long as they stayed safe together, she knew that they were going to make it.

Hearing tires screech away, Abe left Loralye to see the cause of the loud crash. He came back into the room with a hand on his brow.

"The living room window is shattered, and they did something to the car. The windows are broken, the hood is up, and the tires are slashed. I don't think I can justify taking you out in the daylight like this. It just isn't safe here."

Deciding to wait until nightfall, the Wallaces sat with their fingers laced together and waited until dark before leaving their small bungalow. Their silent prayers rose into the unknown. When the darkness overtook the light, they headed out through the backyard as quietly as they could. As Abe held onto Loralye's wrist, they each grasped tightly to a single bag in their unoccupied hands.

"Do you think we are being over-cautious Abe," Loralye asked in a hushed whisper. He took so long to answer as they dodged from one bush to another, that she thought he may not have heard her. As they neared the coast, he finally stopped behind a shrub that covered them and pulled her down to sit and rest.

"I would never take you from home like this unless I thought it had to be done. Loralye, something bad is going to happen tonight. I can feel it right here," He took her hand and placed it on his chest. Her hand was moist with his perspiration. She nearly moved away from him as his heart pounded frantically into her palm.

They sat there together in silence for what felt like an eternity. Loralye tried to ease the ache in her legs while waiting for direction from her husband. He looked panicked, like a deer, not knowing which way to go to escape a hunter. She prayed that the Lord would guide their steps.

Coming up with a plan, Abe said, "We are going to go along the coast and do our best to walk all night. We can find somewhere to rest at dawn and then do the same thing tomorrow. I don't know where to take you Loralye, I don't know how to protect you."

Her heart ached for this man that she loved more than anything. "The Lord is our protector and our provider Abe. Don't take that job solely on your shoulders. Can we say a prayer before we begin? This is going to be hard for me to keep up with your long stride, but with His help and guidance, I know we can do it together."

He knelt back down to her side. "Of course, we can. You know I will slow down for you; we will just take it one step at a time."

Grabbing both of her hands, Abe sent up a plea to his Protector. "Oh God, we need you, now. Please Lord, please help me protect my family. Don't let anything happen to them. Please help us get out of here in one piece, and please stop this evil hatred."

Abe grabbed both of their bags and they left their hiding spot. Crossing the last street until they reached the beach, they raced in the shadows. With each step they took further away from the city, it seemed as if a burden began to ease off of their shoulders.

Walking on the shore for the better part of an hour, Loralye chuckled, shoes in hand.

"Well, we didn't get fish fry tonight, but it's nice to walk in the moonlight with you Abe. I love you." He turned his head and smiled at his bride, his teeth white in the darkness.

"I love you more than anything. You two are my world."

Loralye felt a rush of heat tingle down her body, this man still had full control of her senses.

"What's that up ahead?" Abe said, noticing a light shining in the stillness.

They left the shoreline and followed the brush that was beyond the sand towards the light, doing their best to remain unseen. As they got closer, they began to hear chanting growing louder with each step they took toward the moving lights.

Abe turned towards Loralye. "Stay here. I'm going to get a closer look and see if we can get around whatever is up there."

"Don't leave me here Abe, I'm coming with you," Loralye said in a panic. The darkness felt overwhelming.

"You most certainly are not. You are staying right where you are. You watch the suitcases, and I will come back for you in five minutes tops."

He began to move towards the moving lights, Loralye grabbed him and pulled him in for a kiss. "I love you."

Kissing her with all he had, he then leaned down and kissed her belly. "I love you both with all I've got." Turning towards the light, he ran as fast as he could to the nearest brush.

"Tonight is a night to celebrate. We have six new members joining our district. As your Imperial Wizard, I encourage you all to continue to invite people into the truth! The Bible talks about not mixing, and we will not stand for integration!" The man at the head of the crowd held the attention of everyone who had gathered. His voice pounded through the night with an authority that was unmovable.

"Fellow members, let us join together with one mind and one heart. Repeat after me: In one voice! For God!" The group echoed. "For country, and for the white race!" The group cheered out in a wicked cry of hate, and Abe's knees began to weaken at the evil he saw before him.

The Imperial Wizard continued. "Now, we have a special night to commemorate this historical date. One white man was killed today, and we will not stand for it! Violence is going to be what ends this fight for segregation! An eye for an eye as it says in the good book."

Applause erupted again, causing Abe to move back. His face burned hot when his arm brushed against his wife. "What are you doing!? Go back over there now Loralye Wallace!" His voice was laced with terror, his skin clammy to the touch.

The man in white began to shout, "Death to Blacks! Death to Jews! Death to Communists!" Just then a young man was brought to the head of the crowd, his hands were bound behind his back, and his mouth gagged holding in his screams.

Loralye looked at her husband knowing what he would do. There wasn't a doubt in her mind. Abe wouldn't just stand by and watch. He looked at her, looked at her belly then closed his eyes tight, allowing tears to fall freely.

"I love you more than life Loralye. I want you to turn and run. Run as fast as you can. Go to Elizabeth. I know she has a soft heart for you. Hopefully, her husband is here, or he isn't a part of this hatred ceremony anymore. If I can, I will meet you there."

A cross began to burn, and every member of the Klan, dressed in white, had a torch and was moving rhythmically to the chanting that was being led by the Wizard. "Death to Blacks, death to Jews, death to Communism!"

Loralye looked beyond Abe at the young boy who couldn't be older than 15, as he was being dragged towards a noose in a tree that was too beautiful to be used in such a way. Moss hung down from the limbs, crying out that it already had enough weight on its branches. It didn't need to carry the burden of the abomination being screamed into the night.

"You can't Abe, please. We need you! I love you."

Her hand went to his cheek, unable to keep her eyes dry, she begged inwardly that he would flee with her. She knew he wouldn't. He was too much of a man to do that.

"Run! I love you more than life. Teach my little man about Jesus, Loralye. Tell him about me too if you think of it." He pushed her gently towards the way they had come, waiting for her to pick up speed before he turned and intervened.

Loralye ran as fast as she could, her tears burning her cheeks in the cool night air. She looked back to see how far she had run. The lights were all melding together as one. Unable to distinguish the individual torches, she knew she was making good time. She heard them all screaming and knew that her husband had emerged from his hiding place. "Oh God, be with him," she prayed as she ran as fast as her legs would allow.

Loralye knocked on Elizabeth's bedroom window as softly as she could, hoping that Abe was right and that she would indeed help her escape to safety. Her light went on; "Who is there? I bet it's just that tree playing games with my mind yet again, this always happens when Mr. Kreese is away at night. He needs to spend more time here with us if you ask me."

"Mrs. Kreese, Elizabeth, it's me, Loralye."

The window opened, and Elizabeth investigated the yard in disbelief. "Why Loralye Wallace what on this good green earth are you doing out so late? Is the baby okay? Where is Abe? Do you want tea?"

"Please let me in, and don't turn any more lights on, it is not safe."

An unusual silence settled on Elizabeth before she went into action. "Meet me in the garage, the side door is always unlocked."

Without another word, the window went back into place and her bedroom light was extinguished.

A few minutes later, Elizabeth met Loralye in the garage, still in her night clothes. She opened and closed the door as quietly as possible. "Tell me what is going on Loralye, I am on pins and needles! This might be the most exciting thing that has ever happened to me. Hearing about our poor President has had me on high alert all evening."

Loralye talked as fast as she could, knowing if she took too much time her emotions would take her over.

"We got death threats today Mrs. Kreese, at the shop. Abe came home and said we needed to leave town until things cooled off. While we were packing someone broke our window and slashed our car tires. We were leaving town, following the coast when we came to a KKK meeting. There was a boy who was about to get real hurt Mrs. Kreese, and my Abe went to try and save him."

Elizabeth couldn't believe the words she had just heard. "In our little town, this evil is going on?"

"In your very home Elizabeth," Loralye said, gripping her shoulders, wanting her to know how serious she was.

"Today while I was cleaning the office, the trunk under the window had something sticking out the lid. I thought it was a blanket, I swear I wasn't snooping Mrs. Kreese. When I opened it up to fold it, I saw it was one of those white robes they wear. That's why I was so spooked earlier when I left. I think your husband is part of it, Mrs. Kreese. I hate to be the one to tell you, I think he is part of the KKK."

Elizabeth looked as if someone had just told her that her husband was dead. The life in her eyes completely evaporated into nothingness.

"Are you to tell me that my husband was going to hurt a young boy this very night?"

"If his white robe ain't in that trunk I most assuredly will guarantee it."

Without a word, Elizabeth walked out of the garage and checked the office. A few minutes later, she returned.

"Well, it isn't in there now, Loralye. I just don't even know what to say. I am so sorry that this is happening. He did put up quite a fuss when I hired you, but I didn't think anything of it. We had the money and I have so enjoyed the extra time with the children, I thought he was just being a penny pincher.

My mother left me quite a sum when she passed, and he told me years ago to spend it on whatever I wanted to, so I left it at that."

Elizabeth's mind continued to work, the late nights all making a lot more sense. His little backhand comments, the amens at church all worked together to paint an evil picture that she didn't want to believe.

"We need to hide you. He usually gets home in an hour when he goes out like this. I always thought he was playing cards and smoking cigars; I never would have dreamed..." She lost the rest of her thoughts to tears that she feared were never going to end.

"Come with me. We will hide you until I can figure out what to do."

They headed inside as Loralye prayed that she wouldn't be found by the same man who may have had a hand in harming her Abe.

Chapter Four

Elizabeth led Loralye to the office, where she had cleaned just hours before. She moved the chair that sat opposite her husband's desk chair off the ornate rug and then flipped the thick Turkish floor covering over in a heap. Loralye watched in confusion; unsure what Elizabeth was doing.

"Can you hand me Robert's letter opener Loralye? I think I may need some assistance with this next part."

Loralye moved quickly to the desk and grabbed the gold-plated letter opener from its resting place. Handing it to Elizabeth, she waited for more instructions.

Elizabeth positioned the letter opener between two of the shorter planks that were on the floor. Placing the dull blade at an angle between them, she put pressure on the boards and loosened them. One gave way with a loud pop and Elizabeth cast the letter opener on top of the pile of folded terracotta rug. She lifted the loose board, then pulled up another two, revealing a dark hole.

"You stay here. We need a flashlight."

Elizabeth left the room in a rush, leaving Loralye once again wondering what was going to happen. She sat on the discarded chair in a numb stupor, all the while praying for her husband and her unknown future.

Elizabeth came rushing back in, Eveready flashlight in hand. She got down on her hands and knees by the newly revealed space and shined the light in. Cobwebs covered the eves of the floorboards, and dirt floors covered the four-foot-high space.

"When we bought this house, we were told it was used in the underground railroad. I'm sad to think of this space needing to be used for the very same reason all these years later."

She rushed out of the room again, coming back moments later with a stool the children used to help her make sweet treats in the kitchen. Elizabeth placed it in the hole and then helped Loralye lower herself into the dark abyss. She handed Loralye the flashlight and then left the room again in a rush.

Returning, out of breath, she passed down a chamber pot, jug of water, blanket, and pillow. "You know, Robert wanted me to get rid of this old thing, but I knew we would have a use for it one day. I can't believe I was able to find it to be honest."

Elizabeth looked down at Loralye who was sitting in the dark hole with such compassion, that Loralye knew if she could do anything for Abe, she would. Elizabeth was startled when she saw the headlights of a car light up the office wall.

"He's home! Be as quiet as you can Loralye, and I will think of a plan to get you somewhere safe as soon as I can."

Elizabeth threw the boards back into place, making sure that they were level with the rest of the floor. She then flung the rug where it had been and started scooting the chair back into position. Her husband's car door slammed shut. Giving one more look over the room, she ran upstairs and got back into bed, doing her best to calm her rushing heart before Robert came to bed.

Robert slammed the back door as he entered his high-class home. He took a glass out of the cupboard and went into his office. Pouring himself a glass of brandy, he haphazardly shoved his white robe into its resting place. He sat facing the window, doing all he could to forget the last few hours of his life.

Loralye lay with a hand over her mouth, trying to stay silent. She prayed soundlessly, thankful that her God was omnipotent, that she wouldn't be found, that Abe was okay and that her baby would be safe. As if the baby knew what she was thinking, her stomach began to move rapidly as she was kicked from within.

Robert got out of his chair and started towards the hallway. His foot hit something, and it clanked against the door frame. Bending down to retrieve it he mumbled to himself, "Why are you on the floor?"

He walked back over to his desk and placed the golden letter opener carefully in its rightful place. Leaving the room, he looked it over one last time before heading to bed, an unsettling feeling washing over him.

Loralye uncovered her mouth and let out a breath. She wrapped the blanket around her as tightly as possible, laying down on the hard ground with her head propped on the soft pillow given to her by Elizabeth. What a mess she was in. She hoped that Elizabeth would be able to help her before she was discovered by the evil man that she now laid beneath.

The next morning, Elizabeth made her family breakfast, all the while worrying herself to death about the pregnant woman hidden beneath her husband's study. Serving him bacon and eggs at the kitchen table, she tried to think of ways to bring up the previous evening without arousing suspicion.

"How was your gentlemen's meeting last night dear," she asked as she placed two more slices of bacon on his plate. She sat down to her meal, smiling at her innocent babies as they ate their eggs with laughter, talking about where the eggs came from in an unpolite yet hilarious way.

"Get them out of here Elizabeth, I can't handle the chatter this morning!" Robert nearly shouted as he picked up his paper, placing the thin barrier between himself and his family.

Elizabeth scooted her chair back and took a child's plate in each hand. "Children, I think it is a most beautiful morning for an outdoor picnic, what do you think?"

They both stood up, smiling at each other as they rushed out the back door. Once they were settled outside, both laying on the quilt that Elizabeth had spread out for them, she headed back inside to try to find out something about Abe to tell poor Loralye.

Before she had a chance to ask again, Robert said, "I don't want Loralye here, ever again Elizabeth." He put his paper down and leaned toward her, almost threatening in a way that was foreign to their relationship.

Elizabeth, not wanting him to know that she had any knowledge of the things that transpired the evening before, backed away from him, placing as much distance between him and herself as possible.

"My dear why ever not," she asked, as she pretended to be shocked. She raised a hand to her chest in a gesture of surprise.

He got up and began to pace the space of the kitchen. "It doesn't really matter why I don't want her here does it Elizabeth? I am the man of this house and what I say will be obeyed. Do I make myself clear?"

She got up and went to him, wanting to ease his growing anxiety. She could feel the stress emanating from him. She stopped his pacing and brushed his hair off his face.

"Of course, darling, whatever you want. It is just very sudden. I hate to put her out right before the baby comes. Did she do something to upset you? I thought that she had been a wonderful help here these past few months. But of course, we will do whatever you want. I will call her right away."

24

He grabbed her and pulled her into a warm embrace, Elizabeth's soft response tearing down the wall he had tried to build.

"You did nothing wrong and neither did she. Don't call her just yet maybe wait until the end of the weekend. I just. I just don't want colored people working here. It doesn't look good to the people of the town; I want to be a man that they can trust Elizabeth. I have heard talk around town of people pulling their money from the bank. You know that would be the end of us."

Elizabeth had known her husband's bank wasn't doing the best. She never mentioned it, knowing they would be fine if he would just let some of her money contribute to the expenses. In all honesty, she had enough funds to keep the bank going on her own, but she knew that he would never accept her help. When they married, he made it very clear that he alone would be the one providing for their family.

Everything was beginning to make sense to her. The townsfolk had begun to talk when Loralye came to work for her, and they threatened to take their business elsewhere. That must be how he came to be a part of that wicked group, so he would be seen as one of them. Oh, how strong were the old southern ties.

She held him tightly until he wanted to let go. He pulled away slightly and looked at her in the same way he had when they were just babies, filled with ambition and dreams of a wonderful future together. The look quickly faded and was replaced with remorse and guilt. Elizabeth did her best to mask her emotions, knowing very well where the pain inside of him was coming from.

"All I ever wanted was to make you and the kids proud. I'm sorry for falling so short."

"You haven't Robert, anything that has happened, we can come back from together. Let me help you."

"There are some things you don't come back from." He let go of her, grabbed his keys, and walked out the back door.

Elizabeth watched from the window as John David and Gregory Charles ran to him. Her heart broke for the three of them as she watched Robert ignore them completely and escape to his car. The boys continued to play, and her husband left in a rush, most likely heading to the bank to go over the weekly ledgers as he did every Saturday.

Knowing she only had a brief moment to get some nourishment for Loralye, she hurried to make her breakfast. Eggs, bacon, toast, and coffee were ready, and she also grabbed a blue tin can of Humpty Dumpty Potato Chips and a few cookies she had baked the day before, along with another jug of water, and headed into the office.

Locking the door, she moved quickly to open the dark hole. Loralye stood as soon as the boards were cleared, stretching her legs out for the few moments she had. Elizabeth handed down the meal and traded her jugs of water.

"Are you okay dear? I just don't even know how to say how sorry I am for all of this. I am trying to find out anything I can about Abe. I don't want to come right out and ask so I need to be careful. Right now, the main thing is to keep you and that precious baby safe."

"I understand, this isn't your fault Mrs. Kreeses."

"For the love of all good things, call me Elizabeth."

"Elizabeth then. It embarrasses me to ask, but I may need you to empty this chamber pot if we don't want the smell to cause Mr. Kreese to wonder."

"Oh of course! Hand it up here and I will bring it right back."

Loralye watched as Elizabeth disappeared into the hallway and then returned just moments later with the empty chamber pot.

Embarrassment rose to her cheeks as she handed it back to her. "Thank you, Elizabeth, for everything."

"Of course! Can I get you anything else? I'm not sure when I will be able to get back to you today, so if there's anything at all you need, I need to know now."

Loralye looked down at her little burrow. She had her new water jug, her flashlight, blanket, pillow, and snacks. Unsure of how long she would be spending on the hollow ground, she asked, "If it wouldn't be too much to ask, could I maybe have a book to read? There isn't much to do down here."

"Of course, you can! I should have thought of that sooner."

Elizabeth walked over to her husband's library and grabbed a few books, including an old bible.

"These are from my small collection; I know they won't be missed. Oh yes, and these," she reached into her pocket and retrieved four more C batteries for the flashlight.

"I have more too, so feel free to keep that light on as much as you need."

"Thank you, Elizabeth."

"You are welcome, dear friend. I better get out to the boys before they come in looking for me. I will not forget about you so don't let that thought cross your mind. I'm going to walk to a trusted friend this afternoon and see if she can help."

With that, she placed the boards back into place, moved the rug, and then the chair. Satisfied that everything was just as it should be, she headed outside to play with her sons in body, but not in mind. Her thoughts were steadfast on a beautiful young lady, pregnant with her first child, laying under the floorboards.

Chapter Five

Elizabeth walked with her boys down the road to her trusted friend Anna's home. Anna was much older than she, but they had become instant friends when her family had moved into the charming established neighborhood years before.

She let her mind travel back in time to their first meeting. Elizabeth had been covered in dirt working in the flower beds for the first time in her life. Coming from old money, her mother would never let her do "common laborers" work.

Her mother had since crossed over to the other side, and Elizabeth, ever hopeful of which 'side' that might be, thought no ill of her. Now, for the first time in her life, however, her future was whatever she wanted it to be.

Newly married and riding on the wings of true love, Robert had told her to enjoy their new home while she decided what she wanted to do. She smiled at the thought of his excitement when he had brought her to the oldest home on Cobalt Way as his wedding gift to her.

Charm didn't begin to describe the three-story Tudor-style home. The Victorian gables were freshly painted, the house tinted just ever so slightly with a light blue hue with dark shutters on either side of each window. The brick path invited you to the oversized porch that had two rocking chairs cozied together.

Elizabeth shouted in pain just as Anna was walking by. With a plate of cookies in hand, Anna headed towards Elizabeth quicker than she had been before she had cried out.

"Are you okay? I came to introduce myself, just in time I see."

Elizabeth had one gardening glove off, as blood trickled slowly out of the tip of her finger. What Elizabeth had thought were weeds, littering the ground around her. The frustration of the day wrinkled her brow.

"You must tell me what I'm doing wrong here. I can't seem to touch these things without getting pricked in one place or the other. Where are my manners? I'm Elizabeth, Elizabeth Kreese."

"I'm Anna Court. Please just call me Anna. I'm afraid your first issue is that you are pulling up all of my dear friend Leona's prized roses."

Elizabeth's cheeks rose to a bright shade of pink before she burst into laughter.

"You know, I knew roses had thorns but there were no blooms, so I assumed they were some sort of weed. Goodness knows I have some things to learn when it comes to gardening."

Anna smiled at her and chuckled openly but in a way where Elizabeth knew that she was laughing with her and not at her.

"I would love to walk you through the gardens if you would like. Leona and I loved sharing lemonade outside. She had such a wonderful way with flowers. I can show you what are weeds and what just isn't in bloom at the moment."

From that very first meeting in the front garden, with a plate of the best cookies Elizabeth had ever tasted, they had become bosom friends. Now, as she knocked on Anna's door, she hoped she would be able to solve this pickle in the same way she had done with dozens of issues before.

After the twins knocked on the door in rhythm to "Ring Round The Rosy", the door opened. "My favorite threesome! To what do I owe this surprise visit?"

She looked from the boys to Elizabeth and instantly saw that something was seriously wrong.

"Boys, I have a pile of sticks by the back fence. If you could move them to the compost pile, I may have a special treat for you when you are finished."

Without another word, the boys raced to the back door, ready to take on the task assigned. Anna waited for the back screen door to slam back into place before looking back at Elizabeth. "We probably have fifteen minutes before they are through. What's going on Beth?"

They walked to the dining room and sat facing the window so they could watch the boys work as they talked. Each boy, with a stick in hand, parried and jousted at each other, and Elizabeth thought they might have more than fifteen minutes if they kept up their pretending.

"It's Robert. I'm afraid he has been keeping bad company, and now I am in a situation I do not know how to get him out of." She told Anna everything, knowing she could trust her completely.

After everything was out in the open, Elizabeth waited for Anna to chime in with the unending wisdom she had come to rely on. Never rushing into any reply, Anna closed her eyes and Elizabeth knew that she was praying for wisdom.

"The first thing you need to know is that it is not your job to make sure Robert stays in line. It also is not your fault that this has happened. He may have some consequences for his actions. I just want you to know that none of this is your fault."

Anna reached over the table and placed her wrinkled, worn fingers on Elizabeth's, and Elizabeth nodded her head as tears streamed down her cheeks.

"It breaks my heart that this evil is still going on. Would it surprise you if I told you Leona was from a family that was part of the underground railroad? She would tell me stories of how her Granddad would hide slaves under his study floorboards and then help them escape into safety. She would love to know that her home is still being used to help protect "the runners" as she called them."

"It breaks my heart that my Robert has had a hand in this and that he is the reason Loralye is lying on the ground under our floor as we speak, knowing that her husband most likely will never be coming home."

"You must remember Elizabeth, that we do not fight against flesh and blood. Yes, Robert was a part of the evil that keeps replaying over and over throughout history, but our fight is not with him, but with the evil one who is going to one day, pay for all of this for eternity."

Elizabeth found comfort in this. Yes, Robert had fallen into bad company, but she knew that what Anna was saying was the truth. Her battle was not against her husband but the enemy who thought he stood a chance against her God.

"I may know someone who can help. It may take a few days to get a plan in place. Can you hide her safely for that long?"

"I think so. She is with child; did I mention that?"

"Yes, you did, but don't you worry. We are going to do everything we can to get them both safely out of Beaufort. I heard that the Klan was still practicing its evil ways, but I had hoped it was all gossip. I will call you when I have everything arranged."

The boys walked home with a cookie in each hand as payment for all their hard work. Elizabeth continued to pray that Anna would be able to help her free her friend from the darkness of her hovel before her time of childbirth came.

❧

Monday morning the phone rang, and Elizabeth rushed to answer it.

"Kreese residence, how may I help you?"

"It's Anna, Beth, we have a plan. Jenny, from church, is going to drive Loralye out of town tonight. She has a sister-in-law who is a widow who has agreed to take her in for a time. We must get her out unnoticed. Does Robert still go to the country club on Monday evenings?"

Elizabeth's heart began to race and lighten at the hope that Loralye could be somewhere safe that very night. Excitedly she replied, "Yes, he does. That is brilliant timing. What do you want me to do?"

"We don't want the boys to know what is happening, so after Robert leaves get Loralye into the garage. Have her stay put until Jenny gets there. She is going to pull into the garage and then Loralye can get in right there. Make sure that the door is open so she can pull in. She will never have to be out walking around outside. Who knows who could be looking for her? We don't want her to be seen. What time can you have the boys in bed?"

"I can have them asleep by eight. That should give a window of at least an hour before Robert will be home."

"That sounds perfect. Make sure you clean everything up. Don't leave a trace of anything behind. I will be fasting and praying all day today. Be careful Elizabeth."

"I will be, thank you, Anna."

With that, Elizabeth hung up the phone and began to prepare for what she was calling "the great escape." All day her mind was focused on eight o'clock. Robert came home for dinner, kissed Elizabeth in greeting, and tousled the boy's hair. He did all the normal motions of his evening routine, but he was obviously bothered by something.

"Are you okay Robert? Did you have a good day at the office?"

"Oh, it was fine, fine. I just have a lot on my mind. I know that I normally eat at home, but would you be overly upset if I had dinner at the club tonight?"

Normally, Elizabeth would be disappointed in her husband for not having dinner with the family, but she thought this may just be the grace of the good Lord. With a little too much exuberance she said, "Of course that's fine. You go and have a grand time. We have nothing planned besides a simple meal of meatloaf and mashed potatoes. I'm afraid I burned the rolls."

"Thank you, Elizabeth. I should be home at my normal time tonight after our meeting."

With that, he glanced at his boys, then to his wife, and left with the keys in hand that he had never sat down.

"What do you mean you can't find her? She couldn't have disappeared into thin air!" Robert shouted, slamming his brandy down on the counter.

"Now Robert, these things happen. We didn't want Abe to get involved. He was a good mechanic. One of the new members got overly zealous and started leaving him notes, and then, when JKF was shot, he threw that brick in his window. That must have put them on the run. Always the hero, he pushed that dark-skinned boy out of the way. By then, the Klan was to wound up to stop. They were out for blood, and nothing could stop them."

Robert grabbed Andrew by the collar and pulled him closer.

"If Loralye comes out of hiding and tells what happened, we will all be ruined! Being a part of a group is one thing. Taking the life of an innocent man is another. You told me that boy was a nobody!"

The man put some pressure on Robert's arm, and he let go of the collar he was holding.

"He was a nobody. You saw it just the same as me. Abe ran in to be the hero. They caught the boy, it's just Abe's wife we can't seem to find. You wanted to see more business; I guarantee your bank is going to have more accounts opened this month than you saw in the entire last quarter. We support each other. We are a brotherhood. "

Robert plopped back down at the bar and poured himself another drink. He hoped this was all worth it.

"Has your wife been acting normal?"

Robert looked at Andrew and hissed through his liquor-moist lips. "You leave Elizabeth out of this. She would never hurt a fly."

Andrew took a step back, not wanting to get his collar messed up again.

"I know she wouldn't Robert, hear me out. Wasn't she good friends with that pregnant girl? She worked for you right?"

Robert thought about the past few days. Elizabeth had been acting a little differently. She normally would have put up a fuss about him missing dinner, burned rolls, or not. As if the blinders had been removed from his eyes, he remembered kicking his metal letter opener the night of the meeting, the floorboards! He stood up, grabbed his keys and hat from the peg by the door of the club room, and rushed to dispose of his problem.

Elizabeth got the boys to bed ten minutes early. Relief washed over her when they both fell asleep after only one story. She ran down to the office and helped Loralye out of her hiding place. She handed her a bag with what supplies she had been able to find; a baby blanket from one of the boys, and a few clothing items she thought might fit, along with enough money to start her off right.

Elizabeth went outside first, thankful for the dusk that was settling in. She made sure no one was in view before waving Loralye out of the house. They rushed into the garage, Elizabeth opening the large door for Jenny's car before turning to Loralye to say goodbye.

"Now, Jenny should be here any minute. We are a few minutes early, so just sit tight in the shadows until she pulls in."

Elizabeth pulled her into a warm embrace. "I am so sorry this has happened to you. If I hear anything about Abe, I will get word to you."

"Thank you for everything Mrs. Kreese, I mean Elizabeth. I'm sorry to see our friendship cut short."

"Always friends Loralye, always. I will be praying for you and that sweet baby, daily."

With that, Elizabeth went back to the house to clean out Loralye's hiding place before Robert came home.

Loralye's heart pounded as she waited for her chariot of freedom to arrive. She could not focus on what had happened to Abe. Not yet, not until she and her baby were safe. She didn't have to wait long before bright car lights turned into the garage, blinding her. She stood up and walked towards the door, feeling for the handle, still unable to see clearly.

She got in, placed her suitcase in front of her feet, and closed the door.

"There you are Loralye. I didn't think I was ever going to find you," Robert said with a menacing laugh as he pulled back out of the drive.

Chapter Six

New York, New York present day

Kay Wyley, the Governor of New York, paused the MP3 of her dear friend Brew. He had given his life for her months before in the tunnel of a child trafficking ring, and to hear his voice over her computer speakers brought both sorrow and joy. She wished the story he was telling was a happier one. A tear ran down her cheek, as she listened to the soothing deep voice that was filled with a deep sadness. She hated that he had suffered so much pain.

Kay looked at the clock. It was six a.m. She looked at her baby, Hope, who lay sound asleep in her arms and wondered how she had stayed up all night.

"You are supposed to sleep when the baby sleeps Kay," she said to herself, wondering how she was going to accomplish her tasks for the day.

The door made a screeching sound as her husband Carter entered, startling the baby awake. He looked from one of his girls to the other. His love for them shone out of his eyes.

"You look beautiful Kay; motherhood suits you well."

He walked over to her and kissed her cheek, gently taking the baby from her arms. He kissed Hopes's forehead and began bouncing her gently as he walked around the room.

"Did she wake up early? I must have slept right through it. I was out as soon as my head hit the pillow last night."

Kay let the yawn out that she had been suppressing and stretched her arms into the air. Hope copied Kay's movement as she also stretched her pudgy little baby arms into the air. The couple laughed at the unintentional mimic.

"Actually, I haven't been to bed yet."

Carter's eyes flashed away from Hope to his bride.

"Babe, how are you going to work today if you haven't slept? Did Hope keep you up? You should have gotten me out of bed! I would have been happy to take a shift. You know I can't resist baby snuggles."

Kay smiled at Carter. She was so thankful that he was enjoying being a father. After a car accident a few years back, she didn't think they would ever have the chance to be parents. The adoption of Hope had made their family complete. It was as though he had found his purpose in life wrapped up in the little love he held in his arms. She had never seen anyone take to a baby as quickly as he had, man or woman.

"It wasn't her really. You aren't going to believe what was in the locket that Brew gave to me."

"You mean the one with the fish?"

"That's the one. Come take a look, or should I say, a listen. I have to get ready for work. I'll bring you up a bottle for Hope after I get a cup of coffee in me."

Perplexed at what she could possibly mean by "taking a listen", Carter sat in the seat Kay had vacated. She rewound the MP3 to the beginning and hit play.

November 26th, 1963

Loralye's heart began to pound as the car sped through the city. How did she not notice that this was the wrong car? Her adrenaline had been pumping so quickly she had just blindly gotten into the vehicle. Not that she could have outrun the man that now sat next to her even if she had noticed that it was Robert and not a sweet old lady there to save the day.

She dared a glance over at him. His eyes were bloodshot, and he had a menacing smile plastered on his face. He didn't look right, and she guessed he had one too many drinks coursing through him. The smell of alcohol hit her a little more with each exhaled breath.

Knowing she couldn't try to jump out of the car for fear of harming the baby, she buckled her seat belt and did what she could to protect her unborn child.

"Where are you taking me?" she dared to ask, as Kreese's foot pressed harder on the gas pedal the further they got from town.

"You don't need to worry about that. The town will be better off without another mourning widow anyway. That's right," his cruelty gaining momentum as he continued; "We also don't need another orphan to take care of."

Loralye let out a low moan as her fear became a reality. He had said she was a widow; Abe was gone.

"Shut up! I don't want to hear another sound from you, got it?"

Unsure how to contain the anguish raging inside of her, Loralye held her mouth closed with a tight grip. Tears coursed down her face, and her legs shook uncontrollably. As if to signal that she still had someone to fight for, the baby kicked.

After driving for a few hours, they pulled into what looked like an old, abandoned farmhouse. Robert got out of the car and went around to the passenger door. Opening it, he grabbed Loralye by the arm, and the pain of his tight grip caused her to cry out. She could do nothing but obey his directional pull towards the eerie shell of a home.

Realizing that she had nothing for her child except for what lay in the single bag in the car, she dared to ask a question, no, a plea.

"Please let me bring my bag, I have nothing for the baby to wear when it's born except for what is in that bag."

She looked at the man who held her by the arm, and for a moment she thought that she could see regret in the eyes that gazed back down at her.

"Go ahead and get it, but don't make me regret letting you go."

He loosened his grip and then pushed her arm away from him completely. Loralye ran to the car and got her bag, making her way quickly back to his side. He allowed her to walk behind him without holding on to her. She was thankful for the small kindness.

She could have tried to run at that moment, could have tried to escape. But she knew that she wouldn't make it far, and then what would happen to her? To the baby? No, it wasn't time to run, yet. Retrieving her bag, she then walked back to Mr. Kreese and kept pace with him. Holding tightly to her bag in one hand as the other wrapped protectively around her belly.

The door to the old house opened when they reached the porch. Loralye noticed a light coming from one of the back rooms of the home. She never would have thought someone was inside before that moment.

"Greg called to say you were on your way," the small man said between missing teeth.

"Looks like we got ourselves a little problem here, don't we Mr. Kreese? Folks around here call me Roy," he said menacingly, leering at Loralye as he crossed his arms and spat towards her feet.

Moving out of the way of the brown stream, Loralye bumped into Kreese accidentally. The compassion she had thought she had seen was now completely gone, replaced with rage. He grabbed her arm and threw her into the man who smelled strongly of cigars and body odor.

"She's your problem now Roy. Make it go away."

He pulled out his wallet and handed a substantial sum to the sweaty man.

Walking down the stairs, Robert Kreese headed back towards the car, and despite her fear, Loralye ran boldly toward him. She did not want to be left at this creepy old house with Roy. She was so terrified she could barely breathe.

"Please Mr. Kreese, don't leave me here! I promise I won't tell a soul what happened to Abe. Please just let me and my baby go."

For a split second, Loralye thought he might change his mind, that he might take her back and let her live out the rest of her life with her child, somewhere safe. Somewhere away from here.

The thought was quickly replaced with reality when he pushed her hard in the face away from himself.

"I don't trust any of you. I made my bed, and I will sleep in it a lot better with you far, far away."

Loralye watched him leave as blood slowly trickled out of the side of her lip. She was grateful he hadn't punched her in the belly, the only part of family she had left was still protected for the time being.

With no other options, Loralye walked back up the steps of the old house, grabbed her bag, and went inside into the dark unknown. Roy laughed softly as he closed the door behind them.

After her eyes adjusted to the darkness, Loralye could see that this was no home at all. Cobwebs covered every corner, and a thick layer of dust sat heavily upon every surface.

"Keep walking towards the light. I'm thirsty and need a drink."

They continued down a hallway that led back into a kitchen and dining area. The counters were covered with old food tins that had been empty for who knew how long. The sink was overflowing with filthy dishes, which made perfect sense when she looked at the open cupboard doors revealing their empty shelves.

Roy sat at the table and placed his dirty untied boots on top of a stack of papers.

"Pour me a drink Carmen," he demanded.

Loralye walked over to a bottle of amber liquid, the only drink that she saw, and poured him a drink in the glass that sat next to it. Cringing at the germs that must be lying in the vessel, she handed it to him and said nonplussed, "My name is Loralye."

Roy laughed his awful cackle before saying, "I bet it is. My first wife was Carmen. The ugliest thing you ever saw. I call all the girls that."

He drank the contents of the glass in a single gulp. Roy put his feet back down on the ground, wiped his mouth with his tattered flannel sleeve, and said, "I hated that woman."

"Take a seat, Carmen, Lord knows how long we'll be waiting."

Roy got up and filled his glass again, swirling the contents in a circle before drinking it.

"Sometimes they keep me here for days. Those men don't know what it's like being all secluded in this old house. It's creepy."

Loralye could agree with him there. The house felt haunted if there was even such a thing. Roy yawned and looked at his wrist, checking the time of his imaginary watch.

"It's time for bed Carmen, let's go."

Loralye got up, took her bag in hand, and followed Roy to the other side of the house. He stopped in front of a door, took a key out of his pocket, and opened it.

"Now you listen here. I may not look like much, but I'm fast and I am an excellent hunter. If you try to escape, you ain't going to like what happens when I find you. And I will find you."

Loralye moved farther inside the dark room, moving her bag in just before the door slammed behind her. Dust flew into the air at the motion, and she heard the key locking the door behind her.

Loralye closed her eyes and took a deep breath. She grabbed her belly. She and the baby were safe, for now. Unsure of what her tomorrow would bring, Loralye gathered the few blankets that littered the floor and placed them on top of each other.

She never thought she would miss the dirt floor of Elizabeth's house, but here she was, wishing that she was once again hiding under the floorboards of Robert's study.

Truly alone for the first time since finding out about the death of her dear, strong, mountain of a husband, Loralye cried herself to sleep. In an old farmhouse, with no one in the world even wondering where she was.

New York, New York

Kay brought the bottle to Carter, holding her second cup of coffee in her free hand. "What do you think?"

"I can't believe he left this for you. What a story! Not exactly a great start in life, was it?"

Kay took a sip of her hot coffee as she watched Carter lay Hope back against his arm so he could feed her the warm bottle of milk. She drank the bottle greedily, drops escaping from her lips as she continued to guzzle it down.

"Slow down little lady," Kay said with a smile. She leaned back into the loveseat that now occupied the back of the room.

"Something I don't understand," she said almost to herself, "is why his mom didn't try to get away. There was only one man in the farmhouse. I think that's what I would have done."

Carter looked up from Hope, her eyes now closed, her sucking now more of a muscle memory than effort.

"Something you have to keep in mind though, is that it was a lot different back then. They didn't have phones like we do now or the internet. She was pregnant, didn't know where she was, it was dark, and she had just found out her husband was dead. Where would she have gone if she had made it out of the house? Elizabeth was her only friend, and she couldn't go back there."

"I know you're right, I just don't know how you could sit there not knowing what was going to happen. My heart breaks for her."

"Mine too."

They sat together for several minutes. The silence was not uncomfortable, but felt safe between them.

"What do you think Brew's purpose was in getting this to you?" Carter asked in a whisper, attempting not to awaken the baby who had just fully surrendered to a sound sleep.

"I'm not sure yet. I don't think we will know until we finish listening. There are nine hours recorded on that MP3, and guess who just took her first personal day?"

Carter did his best not to laugh.

"I guess I know what we are doing today."

He turned the speaker down just a hare, slid the mouse over the screen, and hit play.

Chapter Seven

———— o ————

Loralye wasn't sure how long she had been left in the room. She had fallen asleep in a fitful slumber after crying harder than she ever had in her life. Knowing that her husband was gone, that she would never see him again, and that he never would meet his child, crushed her.

Her eyes burned in protest as tears began to fall again. She didn't know how she had anything left in her to cry. Her dry lips sucked in the liquid from her tears like water poured out on the desert sand.

Pulling herself together as best she could, Loralye stood up from her makeshift cot and pounded on the door. She was glad to realize she still had some fight left in her.

"Mr. Roy, I hate to be a bother but I'm awful thirsty and I could use a trip to the lady's room if at all possible."

She waited, wondering if she had been abandoned just like the old home had been. A few minutes later she heard Roy cussing on the other side of the door. He was having a terrible time trying to get the key in the lock.

Loralye's eyes were blinded by the light of day when he finally managed to get the door ajar.

"I swear they make these holes smaller and smaller. Come on out Carmen, I'll show you where the outhouse is."

Loralye followed behind him, Roy using the wall as a crutch every few steps that he took. They went out the back door past the kitchen, and she noticed the empty bottle on their way out.

The screen door creaked open. No screen remained on the intricate wood frame, only an empty casing from better times. Roy plopped down on the ground, hiccupping as he began to speak.

"It's over there. See it? Don't fall in and come right back. I'm watching you, ya hear?"

He fell back against the cool earth and Loralye wondered if he would still be awake when she was finished.

She walked towards the small wooden outhouse, barely making it before it was too late. Doing her best not to touch anything, she looked around the property on her way back towards the snoring mass that lay sprawled out on the back lawn. The overgrown grass almost making him disappear.

Deciding not to wake him up, Loralye sat and started to formulate a plan of escape. She could see fields that seemed to go on forever, and wondered if she could hide long enough to make it to a town and find someone to help her.

Which way would she run if she could? She couldn't leave yet. She needed water, something to eat, and she needed her bag. Resolved, she decided that she would wait until nightfall before she attempted to escape. She sat beside Roy, enjoying the fresh air against her skin.

Roy slept there on the back lawn for over ten minutes before startling awake. He sat up at the same moment his eyes flew open.

"Carmen, where are you? I told you to come right back!"

Alarmed, Loralye jumped to her feet as quickly as her swollen belly would allow, causing Roy to notice her presence.

"Now there's a good girl. I hate it when they run. Makes my ankles ache to run after you'uns. Let's go get us something to eat."

45

He rolled over onto all fours, placing his weight on his palms before being able to maneuver himself into a vertical position. Loralye was glad that he had mentioned food. Her stomach felt as empty as it ever had felt before.

They walked into the kitchen and Roy began to search through the bare cupboards for something to satisfy the hunger that plagued him.

"I forgot to go to the store before I made my way up here. Got stuck with the last Carmen for days and days last week, and I ate all my provisions."

He leaned against the counter, his white, stained shirt creeping up just enough to show his pudgy stomach. He looked up at the ceiling as his finger found its way into his belly button, collecting whatever had been deposited within its deep recesses. He flicked something off his finger as he pushed away from his perch.

"Looks like I need to make a little trip into town. Back to your room Carmen," He held his arm out in the direction of the hallway.

She entered the dark room. Daylight had barely made a difference from the darkness of the dead of night. The only light came from underneath the door jam. He shut the door behind her and locked it.

Loralye heard a vehicle's engine start, and then heard gravel sputter beneath the weight of Roy's car as he left her alone in the old, abandoned house. She wondered how far away the town was and how much time she had before he returned.

Unable to see, Loralye tried to find something to pry open the door. All she could find was the blanket she laid on and her bag. Without any windows in the room, the locked door was her only way out.

Blankets being of no help, she carefully took each item out of her bag. Unable to see, she felt the baby clothes, cloth diapers, and her own folded undergarments. She could find nothing that would help her out of the small room that was beginning to close in around her.

She needed an ax or a key.

"God help me!" She prayed in a panic, as knew her window of escape was slowly disappearing. Defeated, she slowly slid down against the door, her legs crossed beneath her. As she dejectedly ran her hands through her hair, something cool hit her fingertips. She had forgotten about the pins that were holding her hair into place.

She pulled one out of her hair, her heart beginning to pound at the idea of the possibility of escape. She faced the door, kneeling. She straightened the pin as best she could and began trying to get the lock to turn. Unsure how long she had been working at the lock, she pressed on, pushing from the left to right and then from the right to left. She finally thought that she was getting somewhere when her sweaty appendages dropped the pin.

Loralye bent over in a frenzy unable to see more than a few inches away from the gap under the door. She moved her hands over every inch of the floor near her frantically shouting, "Lord help me!" as her hope dwindled away to nothing.

After searching for what seemed like hours, Loralye laid down on the floor, cradled her belly, and cried. When Roy came back from the store drunker than when he had left, he opened the door and handed her a glass of water, a sandwich, and an apple. He gave her a minute to get situated with her meal and then locked her in again, the darkness enveloping her like an unwelcome master.

Later that evening, light flooded in, blinding Loralye as she was ushered out to the bathroom for the second time that day. For this reason alone, Loralye was thankful she wasn't given a lot to drink. The lack of water was the only reason she didn't need to rush to the bathroom every fifteen minutes.

Moonlight lit up the sky. She couldn't remember ever seeing the stars shining so brightly. If it wasn't for the situation she was in, this would be a beautiful night. A cool breeze blew over the swaying grass, and crickets called to each other from every direction.

Roy walked her to the outhouse. This time, he had slept off most of his drunken state and was more aware than she had seen him thus far. Oh, how she wished she could run into the grasses, dive behind a tree, and hope for the best. With Roy right next to her, she didn't stand a chance.

Coming out of the outhouse, Loralye walked a step in front of Roy. He was sporting a rifle in one hand, resting it against his right shoulder. In his other hand, he had a cigarette half-smoked between two fingers, with a new one ready to go behind his ear.

When they got back to the house, a man was sitting at the table. He was just as rough-looking as Roy. He doubled Roy's girth and was a few inches shorter, with a missing front tooth. He reminded Loralye of a villain that she had seen once on the Andy Griffith Show.

"It's about time you showed up Big T. I was thinking it was going to take all week like last time." Roy spat as if to emphasize his annoyance at the long day's wait.

Big T stood up and walked towards Roy, each step causing the old house to cry out in protest.

"Roy, I told you that it wasn't my fault. We had to lie low in the last town. Some hero thought he was going to out us." He laughed so loud that Loralye had to cover her ears.

Enjoying the discomfort he was causing, Big T walked over to Loralye, looking first at her and then at her belly.

"A two-for-one deal! That doesn't happen every day, does it? Do we get paid double for this one?"

Roy walked over to the table and sat down.

"I don't know about that. To be honest, this is the first pregnant girl that's come while I've been working. Course, there's been a few we sowed seed into who left that way if you know what I mean."

They both laughed at their crude joke, and Loralye was thankful they didn't intend to 'sow their seed' when it came to her.

"What's the plan for her anyways Big T? I've been wondering what they would do with someone who was so pregnant."

He opened another bottle of amber liquid and poured two glasses. Loralye cringed at the grime that was inevitably inside each one of the dirty vessels.

Big T took a long gulp from his cup and then sat it down on the table.

"All I know is, she's going to Connecticut. They only tell me one step at a time. You would think after fifteen years they would trust me a little bit."

"That's a ten-hour drive! I wonder why they have you going so far this time?"

"I'm picking up some kids and taking them to New York. I hate kids! I wish they would let someone else do those pick-ups."

"I'd do it if they would ever let me leave this here county."

Roy spat on the floor again, the habit causing Loralye to cringe.

"You know these here woods better than anyone. You have caught how many runaways now? Fifteen?"

"20! I haven't lost a one, except for that one girl who fell into the quarry. Now that was a mess."

Roy shook his head, obviously remembering the girl Roy was referring to.

"Such a pity that was. One of the prettiest girls I've ever seen. Any which way, you're a legend. All the guys talk about how good of a hunter you are. Speaking of hunting, shot any deer yet this year?"

As the men began to talk about the best places to hunt and what size bucks they had each seen that year, Loralye realized that God had spared her and was thankful she hadn't tried to run, Roy seemingly being the hunter that he had claimed to be. She hoped that somewhere on the drive with Big T, she would have an opportunity to escape.

Chapter Eight

The next day, Loralye was released from her closet-room for the last time. Big T came in, his excessive weight bending the old floorboards into a sloping position with each step. Grabbing her by the arm, he pulled her to her feet.

"Time to go. What does he call you?"

He paused, his fingers digging deeper into her arm as he searched for the name in his below-average mind. "Carmen, that's it. Ha, that guy cracks me up. Let's go, Carmen."

His breath smelled of rotting teeth, strong liquor, and old tobacco. She pulled in the opposite direction, reaching for the bag that contained the last remnants of home inside.

"Please, I need my bag. It has what I need for the baby."

"You think you're keeping that baby?" Big T let go of her and laughed harder than Loralye thought possible.

"You get your bag Carmen, wouldn't want the baby to get cold," he snickered.

She grabbed the old bag by the handle and scooted around Big T. He continued to laugh as they headed outside to the old van that was sitting in the gravel drive. Unsure of when she would have another chance, Loralye asked if she could use the outhouse before they left.

"You can if you want, I guess, no matter to me. I ain't cleaning the back of the van again until delivery, so sooner or later, you're going to be using the bucket before this here trip is over."

Cringing, Loralye chose to use the outhouse. She dreaded the ride from the very top of her head to the souls of her feet. After she was done, she took a deep breath and walked back up to Big T and Roy who were talking about a delivery gone wrong by some other no-good kidnappers just like them. Loralye wondered how many people had been taken by whatever group of evil men these were.

Waiting for direction, Loralye held tightly to her bag in silence. When they finished the long-drawn out story of how two children snuck out of some sort of hole and how they were found, beaten, and who knows what else, it was time to leave the old farmhouse.

Big T hit Roy on the back as a goodbye, then looked over at Loralye and said, "Your chariot awaits Carmen. Let's get out of this dump."

He opened the back of the old beat-up van and waited for her to climb in.

All the windows were covered with old boards and the driver's side was protected by a row of bars that went from floor to ceiling. She scooted to the right, putting her back up against the rusty metal that flanked each side. She wondered how long it had been since the seats had been removed. The metal holes were rusted and showed where each had sat. There was a bucket in the corner that smelled of stale urine and she wondered just how long of a trip was ahead of her.

Slamming the door, Big T got in the driver's seat and skidded out of the drive. He laughed as Loralye fell into the center of the van, her protruding belly making it even harder than it normally would be to keep her balance. He laughed, the now familiar loud cackle and said, "You best find something to hang on to Carmen. I don't slow down for nothing."

Folding her legs Indian style, Loralye did her best to anchor herself still as Big T sped away from her last connection to civilization. Fear gripped her when she remembered what Big T had said about keeping her baby. She held onto her belly with one hand as she braced herself with the other.

She thought that Mr. Kreese would never be able to find her now, if he had a change of heart. No one else she knew would know where to look. She prayed a silent prayer that her road wouldn't be long with Big T and whoever he worked for.

After a few hours, they pulled off whatever road they were on and into the parking lot of a rundown diner. Loralye could see through the windshield as Big T walked towards the entrance. He did his best to keep his pants up as he disappeared inside.

Loralye wasted no time. She got up from her crouching position and began yanking at the bars, they didn't budge. Afraid she would hurt the baby if she put all of her weight behind her as she tried to shove her body into the back door, she tried to think of another way out. She sat on her backside and kicked with all her might. Nothing. Prying at the boards gave her no results other than a few splinters.

Screaming for help, her only available option, Loralye screamed with all her might. "Help, please somebody help me!"

She was startled when the back door swung open and Big T climbed in with a vigor she didn't know he possessed. He pushed her against the inside wall of the van and then backhanded her hard across the cheek.

Spitting in her face he said, "Next time I won't be hitting your face but that lump right there, got it?" He pushed on her belly with his index finger hard enough to cause alarm.

Loralye nodded her head yes. She understood perfectly. Her time, their time, was running out. Not moving as quickly now as he had when he had entered the van, Big T scooted himself across the seat, pulling up his pants as he climbed in. He slammed the door closed and backed out of the empty parking lot.

Loralye wiped the goop of tobacco-stained saliva off her cheek before the tears began to fall all over again. Big T got in the driver's seat and drove around to the back of the diner. Loralye was startled when the van door opened, and two men threw in two young children who had their faces covered with what looked like pillowcases.

Squeals of pain and fear erupted out of each of them. Their hands were tied behind them, so they were not able to catch themselves as they were thrown into the van.

"Shut up!" one of the men spat out as he slammed the door closed. Loralye raced to the little one closest to her and helped her gently into a sitting position.

The child winced at her touch and Loralye wondered when she had last received any kindness. After removing the covering from her head, she helped the other child and then worked on untying their hands.

Big T was humming off-key with the radio. His attention was focused on what she supposed was the road to Connecticut. She was glad that he wasn't paying attention to them.

After working on the knots that tied their hands, Loralye was finally able to get them both free. The older girl grabbed the younger and pulled her tightly against her.

"My name is Loralye. Are you two all right?"

The eldest looked at her with fear in her eyes. Loralye figured that the same fear was mirrored in her own eyes as she looked back at the little girl cowering beside her.

"I don't think we are all right at all, do you?" She paused, and Loralye could see her tough outer shell begin to crumble.

The older girl sighed and said, "My name is Cora. This here is my sister Mara. Thank you for untying us."

"You're welcome. Cora, that is a beautiful name."

The girl twisted her sister's hair between her dirty fingers and Loralye winced inwardly when she saw the red marks that went around both of their wrists.

"My Mama said that it reminded her of the ocean. She always wanted to see it and take us there."

She looked from Mara to Loralye, and it was plain to see that her heart was broken when she mentioned her mother.

"Pa didn't know how to take care of us after Mama died. He tried as best he could."

Mara looked up at her older sister and smiled. Loralye couldn't believe that this was happening. Not only to her, but to two beautiful white children who had their whole lives still ahead of them.

"You don't have to tell me if you don't want to, but how did you end up here?" Loralye asked, trying to find some sort of connection between her abduction and theirs.

Cora looked over at the driver, Big T, who was now belting out a country tune so loud, that she wanted to cover her ears to protect them from the awful sound.

"When Pa didn't know what to do with us no more, he found someone to take us. I'm not sure what happened exactly, but I saw the man hand some cash to Pa and then they grabbed me and Mara and took us out the back door."

Cora looked Loralye in the eye as she spoke. The poor girl had to grow up way too soon.

"Pa almost came after us, I think. We screamed for him, and I saw him take a step towards the car before it drove off, but he didn't stop it."

Tears were falling freely now. Cora did her best to keep her head held high.

"I'm so sorry that happened to the both of you."

Loralye placed her hand on Mara's leg, throwing out the only life preserver she had to offer. A gentle touch. She was more than surprised when the little girl left the comfort of her sister and climbed into her lap.

She held her tightly, stroking her hair and singing a song, just loud enough to be heard by the two little girls over the belting attempts of Big T up front.

In Loralye's warm voice, she sang an old lullaby that always reminded her of her mother.

"You are loved, you are home, enjoy the sun as we roam in the woods, through the fields, my little love you're all I need."

She was surprised when Cora scooted next to her too, resting her head on Loralye's shoulder, where she fell fast asleep. Loralye wondered when the two girls had last had a good night of rest and continued her singing in the hopes of bringing them both sweet dreams.

At some point during the long drive, Loralye must have given in to exhaustion. She was startled awake when the van hit a curb as it turned into the driveway of an old brick house. They disappeared into a garage, hiding the trio from the outside world. The garage door closed as soon as the van cleared the threshold.

Big T stretched in his seat, looked into the rearview mirror, and smiled. "Good morning, Carmen. I'm going to go get some shut eye. I'll see you when I wake up and you better be here."

He opened the door and Loralye bravely asked what they were supposed to do all night.

"I could care less what you do. Sleep, scream, whatever passes the time for ya."

"I need to use the bathroom, Big T. I'm hungry and so are these two girls. They don't have an ounce of fat on them."

Loralye was trying not to wake the small sleeping refugees. She wanted so desperately to lay them on a soft bed, cover them up with a warm blanket, and feed them a home-cooked meal to comfort them.

"It ain't my job to feed the cargo. That's the house's job. Sometimes they do, sometimes they don't. The buckets in the corner. Nighty night Carmen."

Loralye continued to protest until she heard the door that led to the house close. Mara started to stir, and Loralye began to sing again. Hoping that for at least a few more hours the two beautiful blonde-haired, blue-eyed sisters would be able to dream of ocean breezes and their loving mother.

Chapter Nine

The house, as Big T had called it, never brought them dinner, or breakfast for that matter. The two girls woke up sometime during the night, their cries bringing Loralye back from the deep sleep she had been in. She had been dreaming of Abe and saw him again running towards his end. She woke groggily, acutely feeling the pain of loss.

"Why is you crying Miss Loralye?" Cora asked. Her tiny hand sweetly wiped away the tears streaming down Loralye's cheek.

"Oh, I was just remembering a terrible day. But don't you worry, we are going to get out of this here van soon. Maybe we can take a walk and get a bit of fresh air. I know I would love to stretch my legs a bit."

Loralye rubbed her thighs, unable to get in a position that took away the stiffness that had set in during the night.

"I would love to go for a walk. Pa never did nothin' like that with us. I don't think we ever left our hometown before he sold us."

Loralye smiled, trying her best to turn the day around for all of them.

"You know, I can remember the first time I went out of my hometown. My Pa was real good with horses. He would train them to race each other, work on their feet, that kind of thing. One day he asked if I wanted to go with him and I was all lit up inside. I was only six at the time. That feels like ages ago now."

The two girls listened with all of their might. Loralye wondered how long it had been since they had even heard a story.

"I love horses Miss Loralye. One day, I want to touch one!"

"Oh, you would have loved these, Mara. When we got to the big barns, we went inside, and there was the biggest black Stallion I ever seen. His mane was as dark as night. His hooves danced around when he saw Pa as if he was saying he was happy to see him."

Loralye felt transported back to the 1940s. She quietly told her story to the two enraptured little girls. For the time being, they all forgot the uncertainty of their future as she continued to tell them about her special day with her Pa.

Loralye had found out why the horse was so excited, when Pa pulled a sugar cube out of his pocket and gave it to him. He rubbed him from his ears on down to his shoulder, whispering something she couldn't hear, like they had secrets to be shared.

"Now Loralye," Pa had said, "This here is Big Mac. He is going to be running a race this weekend and we have to help him get ready."

"That's a funny name Pa," Loralye had said with a giggle. She did her best not to get too close, frightened of the giant beast that seemed to be in some sort of a trance at her father's touch.

"I think so too," he said in a hushed voice.

"Well, you know, his owner is appreciative of the film industry. His favorite movie is called High Sierra, and Big Mac is a character in that movie. The name grows on you as you spend more time with him. He's as gentle a giant as there ever was."

Then suddenly he had grabbed Loralye under each arm and lifted her onto the back of Big Mac. She had felt as if she was a hundred feet off the ground as she looked down from her high steed.

She rubbed him down with one hand while holding tightly to his mane with the other. Pa walked them both slowly to his workroom before he lifted her down.

Loralye sat and watched him work the whole day. She asked him questions about each horse as he looked over their feet, checked their teeth, and gave them entirely too many sugar cubes. When the sun began to go down, they walked home hand in hand.

Loralye was startled back into the present when Mara asked, "Did Big Mac win his race?" "You know he did. Pa let all of us kids go see that race. That was my first time out of our small town. After it was over, we stopped for ice cream with the winnings he got for betting on him. We called it an ice cream walk, and it was one of the very most special things I remember about growing up."

As if on cue, Big T came out of the house and got in the van. He pushed a chunk of cheese and some hard-boiled eggs through the metal bars mumbling something about how he wasn't getting paid enough to do all this work. He waited for the garage door to open, and they continued, once again, on their way to Connecticut.

"Miss Loralye, do you think Big Mac and Big T are friends?" Mara asked quietly as Loralye divided up the portions of food for each of them.

"Oh no, Miss Mara. Big Mac was a beautiful, strong, and nice creature. I think Big T is the exact opposite of Big Mac. Just as opposite as black and white, don't you?"

Mara giggled and took her hunk of cheese. "I sure don't think Big T is beautiful even a little!" Taking a bite, they enjoyed the small reprieve trying not to think about their unknown future.

New York, present day

Carter looked at his watch. It was almost noon.

"I think it's time for a change of scenery. Why don't we take a break and go get some lunch? I know I could use a good cup of coffee."

Kay stretched and got up.

"I know you're right. This story, well, I guess it isn't a story, is it? This evil is tearing me up. If this was going on back then, when do you think it really started?"

"Sadly babe, I think this has been going on for hundreds, if not thousands of years. All throughout history, people have treated children any way they see fit, to increase their own gain."

"Think about it. Pharaoh killed all the babies of the Israelites with no hesitation. They even offered their own children to false gods so they would have favor. Don't even get me started about the evil people who use children for their own gain now."

"When I think about Lilah, our sweet, perfect babies' mother, and what was done to her... and what would have been done with Hope if we hadn't found them in time, it's enough to make a man do something he would end up regretting."

Kay walked over to her husband, embracing him in a comforting hold. Baby Hope was swinging from side to side, asleep in the portable baby swing they had brought up from downstairs. She let his words sink into her soul.

"I understand why God destroyed the Earth back in Noah's day. If it was anything like where we are now, I wonder why He hasn't done it again."

"I was thinking about that the other day. With so much evil in the world, why wouldn't He just start over? But then, I was reminded about Lot and his family. God was going to save their city even if there were only 10 righteous."

"I look at people like both sets of your parents, our Pastor, and you, my bride, and I believe that there is still good being done. Even with all of the hate, all of the sin."

"Don't you worry though. There will be a time when He will come back for His bride. When He does, there will be justice for each and every life that has been hurt by the wickedness of child trafficking, and so many other evil atrocities that our world has deemed as acceptable."

She pulled away from him and smiled. Walking over to Hope, she stopped the swaying motion, picked her up and pulled her close.

"I'm so thankful that we have our Hope with us and that she gets to live a life of freedom."

Carter walked over to his two girls and placed a kiss on each of them.

"We did save her from the obvious evil. But the not-so-obvious evils are sometimes the hardest ones to keep at bay."

Kay looked at him, worry lining her forehead.

"What do you mean?"

"It's easy to look at a tunnel with kids locked up and say, "that's wrong." It's not as easy to look at a bottle of liquor, our complacency, or worldly distractions and say that's wrong too. We must keep our eyes on the eternal. We must keep ourselves blameless."

"I think that it's easy to see the log of sin, so to speak, and neglect the little pieces of splinters flying all around us. We can get so caught up in not running into that log, that we fill ourselves up with tiny bits of splinters that come together and start growing a tree on the inside." Kay was hit with guilt as she thought of some of the questionable shows she did watch, the times she complained about her job, and the times she would skip her time with the Lord because she was too "busy."

"We can do better Carter. There is more we could be doing for the Lord than we are. We must teach Hope that she has to be more than a good person. She has to live her life as a sacrifice to Him."

"Calm down babe, we are. We are growing closer each day and the fact that we see it is a good sign. I have been praying a lot lately that we would not only continue to fight this big battle, but we would also not lose sight of the little battles that come to us every hour."

"Now, let's go get some coffee, decide on lunch, and then we will come back refreshed, then we can knock out another chunk of Brew's story."

They headed to 'Hebrews, She Bakes' for their daily fix. Kay's brain turned over and over the things she may have let creep in during the distraction of reelection and becoming a new mother. She fervently prayed that God would show her how to become more like Him.

Chapter Ten

December 1ˢᵗ, 1963

After many stops, many pick-ups, and very little food, the cargo of three became seven as they finally made it to Connecticut. Big T hummed along off key with a song on the radio. He started mumbling 'Blue Velvet' just loud enough for Loralye to realize that he didn't know the song well.

She imagined Abe singing in his deep baritone voice and wished she would have been able to stop him from saving that boy. Why did he have to give his life for another? What had that boy ever done for them? She was sure he didn't have children to take care of, and most likely no wife either. Bitterness began to build up in her heart. Not towards Abe, but towards God.

How could someone who promises to always be with you allow this to happen? How could she count on Him if He continually let her down? She closed her eyes, listened to the scratchy voice of her captor, and tried to think of anything besides her future.

Looking around at the cramped van, she wondered what all their fates would be. Would they stay together as a group? Where would they go now that they were in the state they had been traveling to? Would she make it to nine months' gestation with all the stress she was experiencing?

She was startled when the van swirled around in a circle, the brakes shrieking to an abrupt halt.

"We made it," Big T said as he spat onto the floor of the van. He looked back and locked eyes with Loralye.

"Now, when I open that door, you all wait your turn and come out one at a time. Carmen is going to get out first."

Loralye smiled at him, this being the first kindness he had displayed since he allowed her to take her bag at the beginning of their trip.

"Then she can help each of you out. It's a bit of a drop for you smaller ones, and I don't want none of you to knock over that bucket of slop. Hear me?"

He shouted the last part as if it were their disgusting habit of choice to go to the bathroom in a bucket.

Loralye scooted towards the back door and waited for him to unlock it. Stepping down onto a gravel parking lot, she rubbed her lower back, doing all she could to massage the ache away. Knowing the little ones needed to stretch just as badly, she helped them out one by one, giving each an encouraging smile, as she gingerly placed them on the ground.

Cora and Mara held tight to Loralye's skirt. The youngest was sucking on her thumb. The oldest waited for the direction of the man that was in charge. He stood a few yards away, smoking a cigar.

Loralye wondered what time it was. The night was as black as she had ever seen it. The stars shone brightly, and she realized that they must be in another remote location. She could only see a gravel road and a dilapidated building.

She saw a car heading towards the little group. Loralye felt the first bit of hope she had experienced since she left the little house, where Mr. Kreese had left her several days before. Or had it been weeks? She wasn't sure.

All the days were melded together now. Time just didn't seem as important as it had been without her Abe. Nothing would ever be the same.

As quickly as hope came, it vanished as Big T waved another car over. Three men got out and began talking to him. They handed him a wad of money and shook his hand as they gave him the keys to their car. They watched him leave before turning to the woman and children who stood there, watching them in terrified silence.

"Now this is what I like to see! Kids who know how to respect authority. You all can call me Toby, or Sir. Those two over there won't be around long enough to learn their names, so don't worry about getting to know them. Carmen, is it?" he said, giving her a brief look. "I want all of you to follow me."

He began walking towards an old building covered in ivy, that looked as if the roof had been blown clear off.

"My name is Loralye Mr. Toby," she said with more confidence than she felt.

The man turned around and took a few steps toward her. Looking from her stomach to her face, he smiled slightly, right before slapping her hard in the face.

The other two men began to laugh.

"I ain't never seen you slap no one before," the pudgy one said between breaths of air.

"Shut up. She's expecting. Even though she is a woman of color, the child might be worth something. Especially if it's female. Now Carmen, was it? I don't want to hear your voice ever. Your job is to listen and obey. You should be used to that."

It took everything in her not to take the verbal bait he was throwing her way. With eyes cast down, hand on her cheek, she waited for him to begin moving before looking up. She tried not to let her wards see the fear that was turning on the inside. With the courage of her forward motion, the seven of them followed Toby.

Walking around to the back of the building, Toby motioned for the two men to move some old crates away from a hole in the foundation. The two then crawled inside, lit a lantern, and called for the children to follow.

Toby tapped his foot in impatience, "Get them down there Carmen."

Knowing it was the only option at hand, Loralye helped each of them slide down to the arms that awaited them below. Mara cried as she pried her fingers off her skirt.

"I'll be down in just a minute. You be brave now."

The little girl reluctantly let go of her hold and eased into the darkness. With the last child now out of sight, Loralye and Toby were the only ones left.

"You have two options Carmen, either you can figure a way to get that rump of yours down there or I'm going to push you in myself. I guarantee that I won't be as gentle."

Knowing he wasn't lying; Loralye sat on her rear and began working her way toward the opening. The lantern was shining brightly from inside, and she could see that there was a four-foot drop. Her legs had been dangling over the edge as she tried to figure out a way down when Toby pushed her from behind.

As she fell in what felt like slow motion, the only thought going through her mind was that maybe death would be better for both her and her child than this. One of the men's fights or flight responses must have kicked in, and he broke Loralye's fall just in time with his flabby body.

"Get this whale off of me Toby, I can't breathe right!"

Toby got into the room with ease and pulled Loralye off him, not bothering to help her off the ground. "You shouldn't have gotten in the way; she would have been fine."

"She's pregnant Toby, I ain't got a heart of stone."

Toby wiped off his pants legs, took the lantern, and began going further into the basement. Cora helped Loralye to her feet, as Mara cried softly, worrying about her newfound friend.

"I'm okay Mara, I'm ok. Let's do what the man wants so we don't get in trouble. Go on now."

She followed behind Toby, doing her best to be the leader these young souls needed. If only she knew where they were headed, maybe knowing her future would help the pain that gripped around her like a snake feeding on a rodent. The unknown squeezed her tight, making it hard to take in a full breath.

When they reached the wall of the building, Toby told the men to move aside some boards that hung loosely on the wall. They fell with ease and revealed a set of stairs that continued down toward the center of the earth.

Lighting another torch, Toby handed one to the man who had broken Loralye's fall and then began to descend the dark stairwell. Soft murmurs began to break out between the seven children, the fear of what was to come hitting them like a rushing wind.

"Carmen, get your group together or I'll throw you down these here stairs one by one."

Unable to see more than a few steps in front of the light, Loralye wondered just how far they would fall before they came to a stop if he did.

"Come on kids, we can do this together, one step at a time," she said with a shaky smile, taking the first step down towards Toby.

Holding Mara's hand, Loralye continued down. Each child followed behind, a light leading the way from the front, and one keeping them close together from behind. With every step, she wondered if the God she had called upon all her years past, saw her at that moment. She wondered if He was going to help her, or if He would just let her die like her husband.

Deciding that she wouldn't ask for anything for herself again, God not being one to answer on her account, she prayed that the Lord would at least keep her baby safe.

Chapter Eleven

After they reached the end of stairs that seemed to go on for eternity, there was a metal door. Toby took a key out of his pocket and opened it, and musty air enveloped the group as they stepped from one dark space to another. Toby stopped and waited for the children who were a few paces behind.

"Now that we are on level ground, we are going to pick up the pace. I expect each of you to stay close to one of the three of us that have a lantern."

The men who brought up the rear of the group worked to catch their breath. Loralye wondered if this would be the time to try and escape.

"Don't even think of running off," Toby said, eyes locked on hers as if knowing her thoughts.

"This here tunnel does have entrances like the one we just came from, but they are all locked. Without the light from our lanterns, you cannot see your hand six inches in front of you. The darkness, along with the knowledge that you can't unlock a door even if you were lucky enough to find one, should keep you close. Understand? I will not go looking for you, so if you run, you will slowly starve to death, in the dark, alone."

One of the children began to whimper and Toby smiled. His goal, to control them with fear, was complete.

If it hadn't been for her baby, Loralye would have taken her chances in the dark. She looked to her right hand and then to her left and remembered the young ones she had been placed in charge of. No, she wouldn't be able to leave, not for herself, and not even for her baby. She knew that she was needed right where she was, no matter her circumstances.

They began to walk down the long tunnel, the children doing their best to keep stride with the men who held them captive. Loralye's head began to fill with bible stories of men and women who were somewhere they didn't want to be for the sake of others.

Moses didn't want to go back to face Pharaoh in Egypt. He complained, and the Lord sent a helper with him, his brother Aaron.

Jonah didn't want to go to Nineveh, but he was made to go in the belly of a great fish. "God, I don't want to complain about what you are calling me to do. Let me be content to simply obey."

Loralye wondered what fears they would face by obeying the will of the Lord. She began to question if what she and Abe had gone through was the Lord's doing. Was He making them face these awful evils? Or was this just the evil of men forcing them into the worst of the worst? She took a deep breath, followed Toby, and prayed without ceasing that God would turn this over for good.

After what seemed like hours, they saw a light coming from the distance. "See that, children? That is your future."

Because of the great darkness, the light was visible for some time before the group finally reached it. When they arrived at the threshold of another metal door where the gleam of the mysterious light shone underneath, Toby and his men extinguished their lanterns.

"This here is a place we like to call The Hollow. Now, do as I say, and you might get the opportunity to eat tonight, understand?"

Without waiting for a reply, Toby pulled out his key ring and unlocked the door. He walked in, not looking back, knowing they all had no choice but to follow.

The smell was rancid. It was as if an animal had been killed, chewed up, spat back out, and then left in the sun for weeks. Loralye would have thrown up if she'd had anything left in her stomach. She couldn't even remember the last time she'd had even one sip of water.

A few of the children lost the contents of their bellies, and Loralye feared for each of them. She held Mara's hair back as she vomited. Cora began pacing in fear of what their future would bring.

Toby kept walking, the smell not seeming to faze him. The concrete-blocked walls were lit by sporadic lights that were several feet away from the ceiling. Brown smears of some sort of bodily fluid etched the sides of each wall at child height. Loralye urged the children on, doing her best not to show her own fears that were causing her insides to flip flop more and more with each step.

They passed several doors before coming to an open room. Some of the tables had blue outfits that looked like prison wear.

"Get dressed, now," Toby said, gesturing to the tables. "Then throw your clothes in that big trash barrel over there," he said as he pointed to a receptacle overflowing with tattered and stained clothing.

It was at that very moment that Loralye realized she had left her suitcase in the parking lot hours before. Tears began to fall as she looked through the blue jumpsuits. Her baby would never wear the little socks and sleepers she had worked tirelessly over. Her baby would never see the wedding picture she had brought of her and Abe.

Loralye worked as quickly as she could, trying her best to find an outfit for each child through the tears. She held one up to Mara, then Cora, then the two boys, and lastly the oldest three girls of the group.

They all held on to their blue jumpsuits, watching and waiting in a sort of stupor. Loralye could sense the impatience of Toby, his conversation with the guard slowing down. She found one that fit her and began to undress, giving the children the courage to do the same.

"Why are you crying Miss Loralye?" Cora asked in a whisper as she put the blue scratchy material over her head.

"You know little miss, blue just isn't my color," Loralye said with a smile that you would have missed if you weren't watching for it. Cora chuckled and put her pants on, first one leg and then the other.

After a few minutes, Loralye presented the children to Toby, all of them quiet and in uniform. The guard, who he had been conversing with, looked at them in awe.

"That here is the first time I ain't had to pull their clothes off kicking and screaming. You got yourself a good group, Mr. Toby."

Toby looked back to his entourage in surprise.

"Well, I'll be. You aren't too bad Carmen. Not bad at all. What room are we going to Thatch?"

"109 sir, want me to have some food brought over?"

"Yeah, that's fine. Some water too."

He signaled for the group to follow.

Loralye stood with her shoulders a little straighter than they had been when they first entered The Hollow. If all she could do was help these children now, at this moment, she was going to do it to the very best of her ability.

73

Tears coursed down each of their cheeks as they walked fearfully into room 109. The sorrow was out of her control, and Loralye's last thought as they entered the room was that her baby was going to be born in a hole, who knew how many feet underground, and she had nothing for him to wear.

Chapter Twelve

The door screeched open, and they saw recessed lights flickering from the inside. Toby entered first, waiting for Loralye and her entourage to follow. There was only one word to describe the room, cold.

The concrete crypt was a sea green color from the middle of the wall up. Dirt, and what she could only guess was dried feces, covered the walls from mid-wall down. The floor itself, was rough and frigid.

Moisture shone on each of the four high walls, as the pooling liquid caused little streams to show a break in the filth as they slowly made their way to the ground.

There was only one piece of furniture in the room. A large bed that was stained beyond recognition. The filth was caked on, as if there was a blanket already atop it, not of cloth, but of dirt and grime. Loralye cringed at the uncleanliness. A single tattered blanket draped the end of the bed.

Toby began to speak when the group had fully entered, still holding the door open with his right hand.

"This will be your home until we decide where you will be going. Room 109 is simply a pit stop if you will. Now, Carmen, I expect you to take care of the children during this time. We don't often collect "product" of your age, so I do expect more from you than just taking up space."

He began to shut the door when Loralye asked in a submissive voice, "Sir, would it be possible to get some hot water and rags? Maybe some soap? I would like to clean this place up a bit if that's all right with you."

Toby looked her in the eye, surprised that she had the courage to keep her head up. Her face was twice its size after he had hit her a few hours before.

"Why would I get you anything? I don't owe you any favors Carmen," he said disdainfully.

"No of course you don't sir, but it will benefit you, sir, that's why I was asking. For your sake." She held her breath, silently praying he wouldn't catch her lie.

"How is it then, that this will benefit me?"

"I'm not sure what you have planned for us, but I guarantee wherever these here children are going, or myself for that matter, we would be much more pleasant to look at if we were clean."

He looked at the group, harrumphed, and closed the door, locking it behind him. A few minutes later, the crusty man they had met earlier, delivered a bucket of hot water, a bar of soap, and a few wash clothes.

"You must have said something awfully nice to get these here lady. We never deliver much to room 109." He left the bucket and walked out.

Loralye tried to hide her sorrow when the man only delivered a bucket and not any food. He must have forgotten. She smiled and tried to be as cheery as the situation would allow.

"Now, children, I know this isn't where any of us want to be. We have all been couped up without bathing for way too long. Let's take turns and wash here, then I'm going to do my best to scrub this place down," she said as she gestured to the room that surrounded them.

"You can't get this clean Miss Loralye; it looks like it hasn't been cleaned since the day it was painted." Mara's eyes filled with tears, and it almost broke Loralye's resolve.

"Of course, we can Mara, have a little faith. Did you hear what that man said? That they normally don't bring things to room 109? I believe the good Lord has shown favor upon each of us, and I am going to do all that I can to put it to good use. You boys go over there and face the wall while us women get cleaned up."

The boys did as they were told, sitting side by side facing the wall. The girls took turns, allowing Loralye to help get them clean. She took the wash clothes and tore them apart, giving each child their own small piece to clean themselves if they were able, and she did the work for the younger ones.

When they were all washed up, they switched places with the boys. After they were all clean as best as they could be with the supplies given, Loralye began to work on the mattress. The water was nearly black when she was done. The dust, and who knows what else, rose to the top of the bucket. The mattress was wet, but much cleaner than when they had first arrived.

She then gave each child a piece of a washcloth and instructed them to go up to the highest point of grime they could reach on the wall and start scrubbing. They worked hard, scrubbing from the middle of each side of the room, working their way down to the floor.

There was a hole in the floor in the corner of the room, and Loralye knew what it was before she got to it. The smell was impossible to ignore. It was basically an outhouse; the hole disappearing deep down into the earth. After all the stairs they had descended, Loralye could only imagine just how deep that was. It was going to take time getting used to squatting and using the bathroom. She would have to help the littles so they wouldn't fall in.

Poring the bucket of slop down the hole, she sat down against the now somewhat clean wall, completely exhausted. One of the little boys she had begun to fall in love with sat next to her, resting his head on her arm.

"Miss Loralye, I'm really hungry."

"I am too Isaiah. We need to pray and ask God to satisfy our hunger."

Loralye brushed the hair away from his face, and his little nose wrinkled with the tickle she caused.

"Does He do stuff like that?"

Isaiah looked at her in disbelief, and Loralye wondered if any of these children had ever been told a single story from the bible.

"He sure does! Now I am going to tell you the story of Moses and the Israelites, and we will see what you think about how He provides for His people after I am finished."

The group all gathered around as Loralye animatedly told the story of how Moses led the Israelites out of Egypt and into the wilderness.

"So, they were very hungry, and you know what God did? He gave them manna straight from heaven! They could pick up all the little pieces of it, grind it up, and make things out of it like unleavened bread, over the fire."

"It just came right out of the sky?"

"It sure did Mara. Have you ever gone outside when it was just light out and the ground was all wet?"

They shook their heads, each one taking in the story that was being told.

"It was like that. It appeared every single day. They didn't have to wonder what they would eat each day, because they knew God would provide for them. Now it's our turn to believe that God will provide for us."

Isaiah leaned toward her; his eyes full showing his fascination. "Do you mean there are going to be tiny pieces of manna on the ground when we wake up? Maybe we should go to sleep now!" He excitedly stood up and started walking towards the bed. Loralye stood as well, her backside needing a reprieve from the cold, hard floor.

"I don't think that it's going to come in that same way, but I am believing we will wake up to something to eat. Let's say a prayer together and then we will all go to bed and hope for the best. Does anyone want to pray?"

Isaiah's little hand flew into the air, and Loralye did her best not to chuckle as he went up on his tiptoes to appear taller than he was. She walked around the group with her arms crossed, pretending that she didn't see Isaiah's hand bob up and down as he bounced in excitement.

"No one wants to pray for our breakfast?" She asked, in mock surprise, impressed that he was able to restrain himself by not speaking out, waiting to be called on.

"Isaiah, do you want to do the honors?" She stopped right in front of him and smiled.

With all seriousness he nodded, moved his arms down, eased off of his tippy toes, and folded his hands, simultaneously bowing his head. The others followed and waited.

"Dear God, I know my name isn't Moses, it's Isaiah. Nice to meet you."

Loralye chuckled at his innocence as he continued: "I'm not sure how you made it do that thing with the manna, but it's pretty neat. I'm not a good cooker, and we don't have a fire here, so if you could maybe bring us some cooked manna for breakfast, I know I's is about starved to death. Thanks for thinking about it, and I guess we'll see if you do it in the morning."

He scooted towards Loralye; head still bowed. Whispering he said, "How do I end this, Miss? I ain't never prayed before."

She whispered in his ear and then he said in a confident voice, "Amen!" The children all echoed him and began to walk towards the bed.

Loralye wished they could all sleep together, but there wasn't enough room. They agreed to take turns and split into two groups. Mara, Cora, Loralye, and a little girl named Sue all lay beside the bed on the floor, sharing the blanket that smelled of urine and soot. Isaiah and the other little boys slept on the bed. They decided the following day they would switch places.

"I wish the lights weren't on Miss Loralye," Cora said, and all the children agreed. As if on cue, the lights went off, leaving the children in complete darkness.

"He does hear us," Isaiah said in awe, and they all went to sleep.

Loralye sat there on the cold ground, surrounded by children who weren't her own and thought of their faith. She fervently prayed late into the night that God would answer Isaiah's prayer and bring them cooked manna in the morning.

Chapter Thirteen

New York, New York Present Day

Kay sat at work with hundreds of emails to go through, a stack of mail on her desk, and a dozen voicemails to return. All the work of the state at hand, and she only had one thing on her mind: the lost children.

She was thankful they had saved some, had caused one of the tunnels to close, and brought light to some of the corruption that was going on. But her heart was heavy with the thought of how many more were still missing, still being tortured.

She swiveled from side to side in her desk chair, looking out the window of the great city she called home. People walked on the sidewalk, dogs barked at passers-by, and the wind moved the branches of the trees to and fro. How could the world seem to go on when there was so much hate at hand?

Unsure of how she was going to be able to help at that moment, Kay got to work, doing her best to stay on task. After calling various charities, setting ribbon-cutting ceremonies in place, and talking her police chief off the edge of early retirement, Kay started scanning through her emails.

She read through each subject, a donor is needed for this or that, come be a guest on our radio show, pray at our breakfast, she was being pulled in a hundred directions. Her heart just wasn't in it. How could she find joy in the start of someone's new business when she knew about Brew's story? When she was reminded of her own and her daughters?

She sighed and continued scrolling. An email from a sender she didn't recognize caught her eye. The subject line said, "Can you forgive me?"

With a quickening of her heart, Kay clicked it open and read through the email in utter shock.

"Dear Mrs. Governor, you wouldn't believe how many times I have tried to write this email. Even now I am unsure if I will have the courage to hit send.

Growing up, I only wanted to be one thing, a teacher. I worked hard and was at the top of my class. I graduated with honors from a good school, and my life was becoming exactly what I wanted it to be.

My mom was the best woman I knew. Her smile would light up the darkest room. She was a giving, joyful, and beautiful person, and I wish that I was more like her.

You may be asking yourself why I am talking to a stranger about my mother. That is if you are even reading this.

You see, If I don't tell you why I did what I did, it isn't going to make sense. If I don't tell you why I ruined your life, you will think I am a terrible person, and maybe have me thrown into prison before I can help you.

My mom got cancer when I was 26. The light that she carried with her wherever she went was gone. She couldn't even get up to go to the bathroom anymore, let alone do the charity work that she so loved to do. She had a rare cancer that wasn't treatable.

There was a new treatment being tested on the type of cancer she had, and I couldn't get her into the case study. There were only 100 spots open, and even though she had the right kind of disease, they thought that her age put her at a disadvantage. *This new treatment was her only hope, Lailey.*

A chill ran up Kay's spine as she read her old name. Who was this woman? She continued to read on.

"I tried everything I could with no luck. I raised money, I donated blood, anything that I could do to show that we were a worthwhile candidate. I thought that if the hospital saw how much of an asset I could be, they would change their mind.

Sadly, they don't work like that. Now I know that hospitals kind of go by their own rules. Data and numbers are what they look for, followed closely behind by money.

The meager $10,000 I made by organizing a 10k run was nothing, compared to the millions they were hoping to make on this new treatment. If they were going to be successful, however, they needed to have their best chance at success, and my mom was not their best chance.

The day before Bliss reached out to me, my mom had her worst day yet. She couldn't sit up in bed without throwing up. I sat there and held what little hair she had left back while she wretched over and over again. She was so weak, so empty. I no longer recognized my once vibrant beautiful mother who had always been the center of my world.

She had been to every one of my games, didn't miss a single parent/teacher conference, and made cookies for every bake sale. She was my hero, and she was dying.

That night when the hospice nurse came to give me a break, I went outside for a walk. It was December and my fourth year of teaching was well underway. A man started following me and I began to walk faster.

My mom lived in a little neighborhood, so I wasn't too worried. I just kept trying to keep the same distance between us. After three blocks, I decided that I was going to confront him and see what he wanted.

I turned around but before I could say anything, he said, "What would you do to get your mom in that medical trial?" Surprised at his unexpected statement, I told him I would do anything.

If I could go back in time, I would never do the awful things I had to do. I never would have caused so much heartache to so many. My grief was crushing me. It's hard to believe, but I also didn't know everything they had planned. I had a small role and did my part and my mom got in the trial.

I know you probably don't remember me or what I looked like all those years ago, but I remember each of you. Every child in my class will be imprinted on my heart forever. You were one of my favorite students Lailey. It doesn't surprise me at all that you are now the Governor. You were always a leader.

All that I was told, all those years ago, was to get my class to what they were calling "grandma's house", and my mom would be in the trial. I had to move out of the country and change my name, but I didn't care if it meant she could have a chance of filling every room she walked in again with her spunk and tenacity.

They assured me you guys would be safe. After I got you there, I was taken to a city in Mexico and given more money than I would ever make teaching. My mom was flown in a week later and started on the trial medication. It didn't work, and she died two months later. I was crushed as you can well imagine.

It was a year before I started looking into what happened in Griddylock. My heart was wrecked when I realized what I had willingly been a part of.

I had decided that I was going to go back to America and turn myself in. I bought a plane ticket for the next morning. Before I left my condo, I was attacked. A man who barely spoke English cut off my finger right there on the sidewalk. He told me that if I ever went *back if I ever breathed a word about what I had done to anyone, not only would I be dead, but every one of you kids would be killed.*

You can imagine the horror of what was going on in my mind. My hand was covered in blood, my mom was dead, and I was risking your life if I came back. I passed out on the sidewalk and woke up who knows how long after the attack in a hospital bed.

I never married, never had children, and didn't think I deserved to be happy. I'm now 60 years old and I want to do something right before I die. You may think that I still have a lot of years left, but last month I found out that I have the same disease that my mother died of.

I should have come back before but to be honest, I have been terrified every hour of every day for the last 30 years. I don't expect you to forgive me or expect you to understand why I stayed silent.

I'm risking my life now by sending this email. I do believe they have forgotten about me. I haven't seen anyone follow me for a decade. I don't have a lot of information, and can't remember every detail, but I am here to help you in any way that I can, as long as I am alive.

For what it's worth, I am so sorry. My mother would have been ashamed if she had known what I had done. She would never have gone along with it if she had been aware of the cost. Now that I know what I do, I never would have either.

I am not able to turn back time and this is the only thing I know to do to try to make some sort of amends. If you want to work with me, please reach out. My hope is that we can work together to catch these evil people before my time runs out. Your first teacher and biggest cheerleader, Miss Craig."

Kay couldn't believe what she had just read. She had forgotten all about her teacher, all about that walk in the woods to Grannies.

Could this be the link she needed to move forward on the child trafficking ring that had almost taken her life?

She opened a new email and wrote back to the woman who had changed her life forever.

Chapter Fourteen

December 2, 1963

Loralye woke up to the creaking of the door closing. She was surprised that she had fallen asleep. Her back ached like it never had before. She slowly moved a child off her lap, doing her best not to wake the sleeping soul who had found comfort in her company.

Moving onto her knees, she pulled herself up, using the wall for support. She was glad they had scrubbed it clean. Loralye found herself missing the ground at the house that she had been in just nights before. Even more than that, she missed her husband's strong arms holding her close at night in a warm, soft bed. She missed her freedom.

That thought sank in. Freedom. You don't realize just how much you have until it is fully taken away as it had been for her. In a matter of days, she had gone from planning a date night with her husband, to widowhood and a four-wall prison cell, hundreds of feet underground. If she ever got out of the mess she was in, she would never take her freedom for granted again.

"Remember the children Loralye," She whispered to herself, bolstering the gumption to continue in the underground box she had found herself in. She walked over to some sort of package that had been left by the door and peered inside.

Tears began to fall when she saw that the box had several small loaves of bread inside. She wanted to wake Isaiah, and the others, but decided it was best to let them sleep as much as they could. There was no telling what the day would bring.

Over the next twenty minutes, the children slowly started to wake up. She gave each of them a good-sized piece of bread, waiting to eat her own until each had been served. When Isaiah woke up and saw what they had, he shouted loudly "Hurray," and woke up the few that had still been asleep.

"I just knew He was going to give us some manna! Didn't you just know it, Miss Loralye?"

He was jumping all around the room, bringing a joy that they had not seen in days. They all began to laugh and clap as Isaiah lifted the spirits of each one of them.

Sitting down with their bread, Loralye told the children another story of God's faithfulness.

"One day, long ago, some men were fishing in a boat off of the shore. They had worked hard all night and had not caught any fish. Now, that's what they did for a living."

"What's it mean to be living while you fish?" One of them asked.

"I meant, that's what they did for work. If they didn't catch any fish, they wouldn't make any money. They had been fishing all night with no luck at all. They were about to go home and give up when they heard a voice from the shore. There was a man who shouted for them to drop their nets on the other side of the boat."

"Even though they had been fishing all night, they did as the man had said and caught so many fish, they couldn't pull the net up."

The children were pulling pieces of their bread apart, listening in awe of the story as they savored each bite.

"How did the man know how to help them get more fish?" Mara asked.

"That man was Jesus, and He knows where all the fish are. He is the one who helped us get this bread we are eating right now."

Mara thought for a minute, pulling another chunk from her bread she said, "I wished we would have asked for some butter too."

Loralye laughed at the little girl's innocence.

"Maybe, we will have to be more specific next time in our prayers. It's important to remember that Jesus doesn't have to do whatever we ask of Him. Sometimes, He doesn't answer our prayers at all."

Loralye thought of how she had prayed for her baby, and for Abe. Oh, how she wished that's how prayers worked.

"How does He know what prayers to answer, and which ones not to?" Isaiah asked.

"You know Isaiah, that is a very good question that many people have been trying to figure out for generations."

"What's a generation?"

"A generation is a period of time. It's a little hard to understand. My grandparents are a generation, my mother is in another one, and then there is me, and finally, all of you."

Loralye knew they didn't all understand, but a few of them were getting the concept.

"I think maybe we will figure it out Miss Loralye. I mean, we did get all of this bread today right after we asked for manna."

"That is very true. Maybe your generation will unlock the code so to speak."

Isaiah smiled and stuffed the last bite of his bread into his mouth. They spent the rest of the morning playing games that

Loralye thought up and listened to more stories she remembered from the Bible.

Although they all were enjoying their time playing and singing and hearing stories, they all had something else on their minds. They were all waiting for the door to open and for Toby or one of the other men to do something bad.

Loralye hadn't a clue at what they were up to. She knew that just keeping them in here wasn't the only reason they had been kidnapped. She touched her face and winced at the pain. She prayed that God would protect her baby and the children in her care.

After what felt like hours, the door opened again. A man they hadn't met before, came in with two more guards behind him. They looked like a trio that had just escaped the local penitentiary. Their clothes were torn and stained, and they all had matching worn shoes.

Loralye wondered if they had ever seen a bath. The smell they brought with them was enough to make you gag. She did her best not to show her repulsion.

The man in charge held a clipboard, very much like the one that the man had the night before. He picked at his belly button with his free hand, flicking something onto the ground that he had dug out of the never-ending pit.

"Okay, let's see here. I think that there should be two of you who need to come with me."

He scanned the paper for close to a minute, sounding out words under his breath. The man could barely read.

"You two big ones, the tall girls in the back, come with me."

The two immediately hid behind Loralye, completely terrified.

"Sir, we just got here. Might we wait another night before we have to be split up?" Loralye asked, keeping her posture straight and civilized.

"No, we may not keep them here one more night. What do you think this is? A Highway House? Get over here now!"

They didn't budge.

"Go get 'em, boys."

The two men came in and ripped the girls away from Loralye. Cora began to scream as Mara was being pulled from her.

She tried to hold on to them, tried to protect them, but there was nothing she could do. They dragged them out and slammed the door behind them. Cora cried for her sister for hours. Everyone was on high alert, unsure if the girls would ever come back.

They sat there, in the quiet, no one knowing what to say. After a long time, Loralye heard one of them say, "I hope I'm not next," and she agreed. She hoped that she wouldn't be next, that she would be able to stay and protect the children that were left in her care for as long as possible.

Assuming it was now evening, Loralye encouraged the children to try and sleep. She sang a song over them. The same lullaby she had sung to Cora and Mara in the van. The one that brought back such fond memories of her childhood.

With almost everyone asleep, she lay on the bed surrounded by little ones. She wondered how long she would have them with her, and if they would ever see the two that had been taken away again.

Cora hiccupped in her sleep. The loss of her sister caused her to be more worked up than Loralye ever thought possible. She did her best to shush and comfort her while lying there staring at the ceiling. The lights had gone off some time ago, causing the room to become darker than darkness itself.

Her thoughts were interrupted, when out of the quiet she heard Isaiah ask, "Miss Loralye?"

"You need to get some sleep, young sir. There is no telling what tomorrow is going to bring."

"I know, I know. I just wanted to tell you one thing. That manna story, the bread we got today, that wasn't my first prayer answered."

"Really? That's wonderful Isaiah. What other prayers have you had answered?"

"Well, really only one more. You see, last week I was praying that I would have someone who really cared about me. I've been taken for a while now, not sure how long really. I lost count a long time ago. I prayed for someone who would take care of me and maybe miss me if something happened to me. Then I met you."

Loralye's heart was brought up into her throat, blocking all the words she might have thought to say in one of the most touching moments of her life.

"I ain't ever had someone who really cared, you know? Then just days later I met you. You don't have to really care about me, but it seems like you do and that's enough for me to think that Jesus answered my prayer. I didn't know He was listenen. I didn't even really know who I was praying to. Now I know though."

Tears were falling down each of Loralye's cheeks as she took in Isaiah's words.

"Maybe you could tell me more about Him tomorrow," he asked with a longing plea in his words.

Loralye cleared her throat. "I would like that."

"Sounds good. Goodnight, Miss Loralye."

"I would care Isaiah. I would care if something happened to you."

She could hear him struggle to get words out. In a choked-out sentence, she heard him whisper, "I knew you would."

Loralye sat there and it hit her. Was she willing to be the answer to someone's prayer? No matter the cost? Before this situation, she would have said absolutely. But now, when she knew the price that had been paid to get where she was, she didn't think, if given the choice she would have been able to do it.

"Lord, You knew the price You were going to have to pay, and yet You sent Your Son to us. Thank you, Father. Let me be as selfless as You were. That no matter what I want, I will be open to being used as You see fit. Let me be what these children need down here."

She sat in awe at being someone's answer to prayer. She hoped that God was going to continue to answer their every need. She prayed for the two children that had been taken from them, and hoped and prayed that tomorrow would bring them back to her. With no energy left, she closed her eyes and fell asleep.

Chapter Fifteen

The next morning was filled with sorrow when the two girls who had been taken the day before still had not returned. Loralye wanted to do something, to speak to someone, but she didn't know how or who to talk to. Sweet Cora was inconsolable.

"There now child, dry up those tears. We need to keep praying for Mara. Pray that God keeps her safe and brings her back to us."

She stopped crying for a moment, and Loralye could tell she was pondering something important in that sweet little head of hers. Then the floodgates returned, and between sobs, she said, "What if God don't answer me?"

Loralye sat with her on the edge of the bed and rocked her back and forth. "There now, don't let that doubt sink in young one. We need to believe that He will. We also have to remember that He is in control."

Loralye was speaking to her inner soul just as much as she was talking to the girl. Was she willing to completely surrender to God's will? Was she okay with God using her to answer Isaiah's prayer? She hoped she could get there someday.

As the day went on, Loralye did her best to keep the group busy. She decided she was going to ask whoever came through that door next, for another bucket of water and some soap. The stains on the bed were better, and it didn't smell unbearable, but the room was far from clean.

As if the men had read her mind, the door swung open. Loralye's courage left just as quickly as it had come. She instinctively placed her arm around Cora in a protective manner as if to say, "You can't have her," with her body.

There was only one man this time, and Loralye hoped that was good news. It was the same man as the day before, clipboard in hand. "I need to take you, Carmen, I think it says, to have a little meeting with Toby."

Cora grabbed ahold of Loralye's arm, holding on with all her might. Loralye whispered to her, "I'll be back. There is only one man this time. They don't mean to take me away from here for long."

She stood up and lifted Cora from the bed. Placing her on Isaiah's lap, she smiled at him. He shook his head, letting her know that he would keep watch while she was away. Walking to the open door, Loralye went out into the hall and waited for the man to lock it.

He bumped into her as he took the lead.

"You follow me now. Don't make me wait for you, ya hear?"

He continued to walk down the long hall at a snail of a pace. Loralye thought that if they were to have a foot race, she would beat him pregnant or not. If only she knew how to get out of here.

Deciding that it would be more beneficial to take in as much as she could than stare at the fat man ahead of her, Loralye examined everything. The walls appeared to be cement. They were filthy just as their room had been, from four to five feet up, all the way down to the ground. She hated the thoughts that came into her mind on how and what that grime was.

There were lights hanging every six feet from the high ceilings. No natural light, which she figured, seeing as they went down so many stairs to get there. Every twenty or so feet there was another door just like hers. She hoped they didn't have children locked in them too.

They turned and went down another long hallway that was almost identical to the one they had just left. The only difference was the screams she heard coming from the new hallway. She cringed inside and prayed that Mara wasn't the owner of any such howl.

They continued to walk, and the tunnel went on and on. After at least ten minutes, they stopped at a door that looked identical to all the others. The man knocked twice and walked in, not waiting for an invite.

"I got her, just like you wanted Boss. Do you want me to stand guard?"

"Not necessary. Come back in half an hour."

With that, the man exited, closing the door a little harder than he needed to. The thick metal door muffled the torturous screams until they were indistinguishable. Loralye was remorseful that she was relieved when she could no longer hear them.

"Take a seat, Carmen," Toby said, as he searched for something on his desk. Loralye reluctantly took a seat, easing her back against the soft backing. She tried not to let it show that she was enjoying the back support. Knowing the man who had brought her there was coming back for her soon, put her mind at ease. She would be returning to the children, just as she had thought.

"Carmen, we have never had a room stay as quiet as you have been able to accomplish with the group in 109. My superiors and I have been talking, we have decided to give you a position here at The Hollow."

Loralye wanted to shout, yell, and slap the man for ever thinking that she would work for him. A still small voice told her from within to *stay silent.* She took in a breath and waited for him to continue.

"Now this may not be a permanent position, but for now, we are willing to give it a go, and see if it improves our worker's jobs of wrangling the merchandise. The job isn't going to be easy."

He paused, and glanced up from his desk, looking at her swollen face, locking eyes with her, and she thought she saw regret within them. He leaned closer to her, talking to her in a hushed manner as he continued on.

"Loralye, if you do not take this position, I can guarantee that you will not see your child for more than a few hours after it's born."

She began to shake as he sat back and began to give her the job description. She knew before he started that she would be taking it.

"Now, we are going to count on you to help the new groups get settled in their rooms, along with some cleaning. Even doing the basics you did in room 109 will suffice, for now. After you give birth, we will require more from you."

She never once broke her gaze on Toby. She wouldn't cower away, no matter how much she wanted to. He looked away in discomfort. Clearing his throat, he carried on.

"I have been told that if you can keep the children calm, you can keep your son with you for a time."

"How long?" She said louder than she had intended to.

"I can't guarantee anything."

They sat in silence for several minutes. He shifted uncomfortably and went on. "I know that as your time draws on, lifting things is going to become more cumbersome. We have decided to let one child help you until after the baby is here."

"Can I choose who that is?"

He thought about it for a moment. He wasn't used to anyone down there asking things of him, and he admired her courage.

"I suppose I can allow it. I would encourage you to pick someone who will aid you in your demands. If this doesn't work out, let's just say we will move forward with the same plan we had for you before this idea was formulated."

"May I ask what those plans were?"

"You don't want to know."

She believed him.

"You will have tonight to decide who you want to be your helper, and then your work will start first thing in the morning."

He stood up, signaling that the meeting was over. Walking to the door, he opened it and looked for the man who had brought her to him.

"Porker," He yelled, and the man came running from around the corner. If the circumstances hadn't been so bleak, she would have laughed at the resemblance the man had to his name.

"I will have something drawn up for you tomorrow. You can read, can't you?"

"Of course, I can."

"I thought so. You wouldn't believe the number of people who come through here who can't."

He looked pointedly at Porker who was swatting at a spider climbing up the wall. He waved them off, not bothering to hide his annoyance at the simple-minded man, and walked back towards his desk, continuing on with what he had been doing before Loralye had arrived.

She followed Porker back the way they had come to the cell with the children she was falling in love with a little more each day. She wondered how she was ever going to be able to choose her helper, knowing the fate of the others was going to be anything but good.

Chapter Sixteen

T he children were relieved to see Loralye when she came back to them. Cora ran from Isaiah and threw her arms around her legs. "I didn't think you were coming back Miss Loralye."

Loralye hugged her back. Her emotions were threatening to spill over once again. She looked at all the children who were in the room and wondered, again, how on earth she was supposed to decide who was going to help her with her new job.

"Lord, I don't know how I am ever going to do this," she prayed silently. Looking from one child to the next, she didn't want to risk losing any of them.

"I will help you," she heard whispering back. Taking a deep breath, she smiled and walked over to where the children had been sitting on the floor.

Looking back towards the door, Porker was still trying to figure out the lock and key situation which was utterly ridiculous. He had just unlocked the door, why did he ever pull the key from its place? Deciding it may be a blessing from the Lord, Loralye tried not to chuckle at the childlikeness that was evident in the incompetent man.

"Porker, do you think we might get something to eat today?" She asked in the friendliest voice she could.

Dropping the keys from his hands, he hurried to pick them back up.

"I don't know Carmen; I don't normally bring food to the kids." He continued to look for the correct key, giving Loralye more time to try to persuade him.

Encouraged that he had called the group children, and not something as demeaning as merchandise, Loralye thought that he could be just the person they needed for sustenance.

"I'm sure that your job is much more important than running around bringing people food," she said, noticing the man-child's posture straighten with the praise. She went on, "We would be very thankful for anything that you could bring. I saw how fast you ran when Toby called for you. I don't think it wouldn't take but a minute or two for you to get it."

"I am real fast Carmen," he began excitedly. "One time, I caught this boy who had gotten out of the chains in the scare room. No one else could grab him, but I snatched him out of nowhere." He smacked his hands together as he told his heroic tale, scaring all the children simultaneously.

"I am sure that was a very exciting day," Loralye said as if praising a child.

"I bet, if you wanted to, you could go just as fast to get us some dinner. The children and I will all count and see just how fast you are."

Loralye hoped that the children's game she had played with the Kresse's' twins would work.

He thought about it for a moment before he said, "Okay, but I'm not going to need long at all! I do have to lock the door first, so don't start counting until I say go." He went out into the hall and locked the door. Loralye chuckled, seeing that the man had been stalling all along.

"I'm ready Carmen!" He yelled through the door.

"Ready, set, go!" Loralye shouted and hoped that he would indeed bring them all back something to eat.

"Okay, children let's count! One, two, three. ." they all counted together, and their excitement increased as the numbers grew.

When they reached one hundred, Loralye's faith began to wane. How high should she count before admitting defeat? They continued. .

"One hundred and ten," she was counting alone now. The children had stopped long ago. Not because they weren't excited about a meal that may or may not be coming, but because they didn't know which numbers came next.

She continued, until Isaiah shot up from his sitting position. "I hear keys! Miss Loralye, he came back!"

The children began to shout in excitement, waiting for the door to open, they all began to chant together, "Porker, Porker, Porker."

The man came in winded more than he should have been. Loralye was relieved that his arms were filled with food. He dropped a loaf of bread along with the keys as he pushed open the door. Isaiah ran over and picked up the meal.

A normal child who was starving would open the loaf and take a bite, but that wasn't what Isaiah did. He picked it up and handed it back to Porker so that he could give the gift of food to the children himself.

Porker smiled and took his loot to the bed that had been vacated by the excited children and laid it all out.

"I was a little slow, but I'll do better next time. I got a loaf of bread, a jar of peanut butter, and some cheese. We get to eat as much as we want here, and I had all this back at my desk."

Mara and one of the younger boys named Jay ran up and hugged Porker, holding tightly to each leg. The boy went as far as kissing him on the calf.

"Your legs are so fast! Peanut butter is my favorite!" Letting go, he went over to the bed.

Loralye smiled at the sweet moment, receiving Mara back into her arms. For the first time since being down in The Hollow, she wondered what sort of life the guards had lived. Had they ever been loved? She didn't think compassion was something well-known down there.

Porker began to walk towards the door, and she followed him.

"Porker, would you like to share a peanut butter sandwich with us? There is plenty here."

He turned to face her, surprised by the invitation.

"Carmen, no one has ever hugged me before." Guilt washed over him. He took a deep breath and went on.

"They won't like me too much longer. This place isn't good," he said in a hushed voice, hoping the children wouldn't hear him.

"I know it isn't," Loralye said, unsure of what else to say. They shared a moment by the door in the cement room while the children giddily laughed over the peanut butter and cheese. The excitement was tangible, and he smiled.

"Thank you, Porker."

"Yeah, it was nice to make someone smile for a change."

With that, he left the room, locking the door behind him.

Loralye walked over to the bed, watching little Jay jump up and down with excitement. "Can we eat now Miss Worawye?"

"Yes, we can young man. Are you hungry?" He shook his head yes as Loralye picked up the block of cheese and began to break it apart.

"Can we pray before we eat Miss Loralye? I just don't want to not thank God for all of this," Isaiah said pointing to the food.

"That's a great idea, why don't you go ahead."

"Bow your heads guys," Isaiah said, looking around at the small group. He waited patiently until each one had bowed their head, and then he bowed his own.

"Dear God, we know that you can bring manna, that's bread, and you can tell people where to fish, but peanut butter? I didn't even think they had that when you were alive. Jelly would have been great, but we like this too, thank you. Amen."

"Amen," the group said excitedly. Isaiah helped Loralye pass out a sandwich to everyone sitting in the circle. He took his right before Loralye, knowing she wouldn't eat until he had something for himself. As he took the first bite of his sandwich, the others were taking their last. He broke off a piece of his sandwich and gave it to Jay. The compassion that he had for others was all she needed to see. She knew then that he was the one she would choose to help her.

Chapter Seventeen

The next morning, Loralye was again summoned to speak with Toby. She knew she had to give him an answer and even though she knew what that answer was, she couldn't help but feel that it was her fault that the others wouldn't be able to stay with her. That because of the decision she had to make, she wouldn't be able to protect them any longer.

Porker knocked on Toby's office door and waited until he heard his voice before he opened it.

"Thank you, Porker. Come back in half an hour," Toby said, briskly.

His tone did not match his words of thankfulness. He reminded Loralye of a child who had been taught that if he didn't say thank you, he wouldn't be allowed dessert.

Loralye sat in the same chair she had been in the day before, unable to relax back into the cushion. The weight of her decision began to press down further and further with every passing moment.

"*Lord, if this isn't the right decision, please speak to me now,*" she said inwardly, knowing that she was almost out of time.

Toby leaned back and lit a cigarette. He blew out the smoke away from the woman across from him, and Loralye thought that maybe the man in front of her had some goodness in him after all. Using the ashtray in front of him, he asked her the question she had been thinking about all night.

"Well, have you made a decision? Who will you choose to help you?"

Taking a deep breath, Loralye sat up as straight as she could in her seat. "I have sir."

"Well, who is it going to be?"

"Would it be possible for me to have two children to help me? We would be able to move a lot quicker through the rooms." Everything within her hoped that he would comply, and she held her breath as she waited for his answer.

"No."

She had to try. The thought of leaving Mara behind caused an ache deep in her bones. Doing her best not to show him the anguish she felt, she said, "I would like Isaiah to help me."

Toby extinguished his cigarette before responding. He folded his hands into each other and swiveled from side to side in his chair.

"You surprise me more and more every day Carmen. I thought for sure you would choose the little blonde thing that holds on to you tighter than a leather glove."

Loralye didn't shy away from the man. Looking him straight in the eye, she let him know exactly what she thought of the situation.

"No child should have to be spending their time cleaning up feces and smears of blood. The fact that this is their story, and mine, doesn't feel right. I feel like we are in an impossible nightmare."

She took a breath and went on, "I am thankful for the help, but it is an impossible task to choose one child to live, while several others may die."

He looked at her in wonder. He was more impressed with her understanding of what was going on than he cared to admit.

"Do yourself a favor and don't look at them as children. Think of this place as a laboratory, or a feedlot. Everyone has a purpose to fill, a need to meet. We just facilitate a product that most people aren't accustomed to buying."

"How can you possibly become accustomed to looking at a child the same way you look at a cow?" She slammed her hand hard against the desk that separated them. The righteous anger that had been building up inside of her ached to be let out.

"Watch how you talk to me, Carmen. You're riding a fine line here, and it would only take the snap of my fingers to have your fate sealed in a much darker way than scrubbing toilets, understand?"

Unable to hold his gaze, Loralye meekly said that she understood.

"Perfect. I do believe Isaiah was a wise choice. You are going to need muscle to lift the water bucket and supplies. I'm going to have Porker show you around the rooms I want you to start in. You and the boy will be moved to a smaller room tonight."

Toby got up and walked towards the door. He opened it and waited for Loralye to exit the room.

"Walk down that way and you will find Porker. He's probably in the mess hall eating something."

She began to walk in the direction he had instructed.

"One more thing. If you ever hit my desk again, or anything else for that matter, I will wash my hands of you." He slammed the door and left Loralye alone in the hallway.

She stood there for a moment before running to the first door to her right. As she turned the knob, she wasn't surprised to find that it was locked. She ran to the next door, and then the next, but each one was locked as tight as a door can be. She gave up after trying to open half a dozen doors and finally, slowing to a walk, she worked her way down the hall towards Porker.

Sure enough, she found him several doors down. The room was the only one open. Several men sat playing cards at a far table in the back of the room. Porker stood with a plate filled to overflowing, looking over each man's hand of cards.

"That there's a good pair you got Steve."

Steve turned in his seat and flipped the plate of food out of Porker's hands.

"Porker, you better get out of here before I punch you in that big, fat gut of yours!"

Porker must have known the man wasn't bluffing. He took several strides towards the door, afraid to look away from Steve until he was far enough away to feel safe. He turned around just in time to see Loralye before bumping into her.

"Done already huh? Let's get out of here. No one appreciates a compliment anymore."

They walked further down the monotonous hall, Porker whistling all the while. They stopped at a door and Porker fumbled with his keys, searching for the right one.

"Now this here is the supply closet. We keep the buckets and cleaning supplies in here. We don't use it much. Toby said to have you make a list of what you need."

He opened the door and turned the light on. Loralye entered the small room and took note of what was available. There were three metal shelves filled with different bottles of various chemicals. The disorganization of the room made Loralye believe there hadn't been a woman down in the tunnels for quite some time.

"Well, what will you need Carmen?" Porker asked, leaning against the door jamb.

"Do you think I could go through these shelves and take an inventory of what's in here? It might take some time to get this all sorted out so I can see what I need."

"Yeah, that's fine. Toby said you'd probably spend some time here. He told me to tell ya that you have to get a room cleaned today too. So, don't take too much time in here. I'll be back. I'm going to see who's winning at cards." He left before Loralye could answer.

She marveled at the trust these men had. What was to keep her from running off? Thinking of all the locked and look-alike doors, Loralye realized it wasn't that they trusted her, but that they trusted their security. She got to work, removing each item off the shelves, and putting things into categories.

Toby came back sometime later, his whistling announcing his arrival. Loralye stood up from her crouched position, with a piece of paper in hand.

"I found a pad of paper with a pencil in the binding of an empty bucket. Here is a list of things I need. I put the more important things at the top of the list."

Porker took the paper and put it in his pocket without looking at it. She figured he wouldn't be able to read the list even if he wanted to.

"This looks pretty good Carmen. I didn't even know we had a broom down here. Learn something new every day."

Loralye grabbed the two bags of trash she had collected from the shelves. Almost every bottle on the shelves had been completely empty.

"Where can I take this trash, Porker?"

"I'll take you to the incinerator. We burn all our trash down here."

They walked for a few more minutes. Finally, turning down another hall, they stopped in front of a door that was twice as wide as all of the others.

"The door makes it easy to spot. Toby is going to get you a key for this door and the supply door. I will take you to the rooms they want you to clean every day."

"Thank you," she said as she waited for him to unlock the double-sized opening.

"The fire is only turned on at night. You can leave your daily trash here and someone will throw it in when they get everything fired up."

"Why don't they run it during the day" she asked as he threw the bags onto the pile next to others that were collecting near the large open oven.

"Oh, it's so no one will see the smoke coming up. We are out in the boonies, but we do our best to stay secret-like."

Porker walked her back towards room 109 talking nonstop about Steve and his winning hand.

Loralye did her best to pay attention, but her feet and back ached from both the work and their sleeping situation. Stopping at their door, Porker unlocked it and let her in. Not staying to chat, he shut the door behind her.

Loralye looked up from her shoes and saw only one child sitting alone on the bed. Isaiah looked up with tears in his eyes.

"They took them Miss Loralye, they came and took them all.

Chapter Eighteen

Loralye held Isaiah close. They cried for each of the children who were behind one of the many doors in the desolate Hollow where they were imprisoned. She prayed that God would do something, that He would move mountains to save the little ones she could not.

The door opened a few hours later and Porker stood with a bucket in hand and a smile on his face.

"I have your first assignment. Room 218 needs to be cleaned and ready for tonight's drop-off." Isaiah looked from Porker to Loralye.

"What's going on Miss Loralye? Are they going to take me too?"

Loralye could feel fear radiate from him as panic began to settle in at the thought of being taken away. In the softest voice she could muster, she whispered; "Isaiah do not let fear fill you up now. They aren't taking you. We have work to do! God has placed us here to do a special job. Are you going to be able to help me?"

He began to calm down at her words. After a few breaths, he said, "I will try Miss Loralye."

"Good. Let's go clean room 218."

They got up and headed to the door. Porker handed the bucket to Isaiah and began to lead them down the tunnel.

"This room is bigger than yours. I'll show you where to get water for the cleaning. I found a few containers of bleach Carmen. I put them in your closet."

Loralye held Isaiah's free hand as they followed behind Porker.

"Thank you, Porker. Bleach will help tremendously with all the germs down here."

"I don't know what that tremendous thing is, is it a lot?"

"Yes, it's a whole lot."

He stood straighter as they continued to walk the halls. He stopped at a door and let them in to fill the bucket with water. The room had a concrete floor with a drain surrounded by a buildup of concrete to form a makeshift tub of sorts to dump the water down.

Isaiah placed the bucket under the faucet and began to fill it. Realizing they had hot water, Loralye cranked the knob in the opposite direction.

"Praise you, Lord!"

She took one of the washcloths out of the bottom of the bucket and soaked it under the scalding water. She scrubbed her face and enjoyed the first real warmth she had felt since she had arrived.

Giving one to Isaiah, they both scrubbed down their arms and hands as the bucket filled. When it was just over half full, they put their washcloths in the bucket of warm water and carried it together. Loralye watched as the rags slowly sank to the bottom of the bucket as they followed Porker to the supply closet. After getting one of the containers of bleach, they walked slowly to room 218.

Water sloshed and spilled over, getting Loralye and Isaiah's pants wet with the overflow. Porker stopped at another door and opened the unlocked room.

"Here it is. I will be back in a few hours. They are moving the two of you to another room, so don't go back to 109. Here is the key to the water closet, and the supply closet. You can go back and forth as you need to." With that, he left the two alone.

Isaiah looked at Loralye with wide eyes filled with hope. He didn't have to say what he was thinking, Loralye already knew.

"We can't run Isaiah. All of the doors are locked. I tried." Knowing that she was right, he followed her into the room.

The space was much like theirs had been the day they had arrived. The only difference was the double bunkbeds that were on the far wall. Unsure of when more supplies would be given, Loralye dumped half a cap of bleach into the bucket of water. Putting her arm down into the warm liquid, she stirred it around and thanked the Lord she would have a way to get rid of some of the germs that lined the walls.

Isaiah walked around, examining the large room. Besides the beds, small sink, and the hole in the ground to use as a toilet, it was empty. He noticed there were no blankets on the bed.

"Miss Loralye, do you think they had a blanket when they were here?"

"I don't know Isaiah, I hope that they did."

"Me too. We could have given them our blanket."

"We could have. You have to remember though that there were small children in the room with us too, and we had to take care of them as well."

He paused at that and thought about the words she had said.

"We were taking care of other little kids, weren't we?"

He walked over to the bucket, wrung out one of the rags, and began to scrub the far wall.

Loralye took a rag and joined him. They worked together, scrubbing the walls, and emptying the buckets after each one. The water was black as it swirled down the drain. After the walls were wiped down, they took the mattresses off the bunks and did their best to get the top coating of muck off of each of them.

Porker returned just as they were placing the last mattress on one of the bunks. He walked in with his arms crossed. Pulling one of his hands to his chin, he went around the perimeter of the room as if he were a foreman, inspecting their work.

"Well, I see a few things here and there, but it will do. Come on now, I'll show you your new room."

They walked back towards the supply closet and put their things away so they would be ready for the next day. They walked back down towards room 109, as Porker talked about all the ways they might improve their job.

Loralye did her best not to laugh out loud when he suggested they scrub harder by the legs of the bed. You couldn't scrub away the permanent marks on the concrete floor where the bed had been rubbing.

Passing dozens of rooms, they finally stopped at room 89.

"This is your room for now. Toby said I could bring you dinner when you were finished. I'll be back." He left them to go inside alone.

The room was small but surprisingly clean. A single bunk sat along one wall. There was a sink and the customary hole in the ground to use the restroom. A wooden chair sat in a corner, and Loralye was beyond thankful to have somewhere she could sit with back support that wasn't the floor.

Porker came back in, with his arms full. Loralye and Isaiah rushed to help him unload the items he carried. His face beamed with a bright smile.

"I have been looking all day to find stuff for you to make this place like home."

Loralye couldn't help but care for this "man-child", despite his role in this dark place. It was obvious that he had never been cared for, and was trying, maybe for the first time, to care for someone else.

He had brought two thin blankets, a jar of peanut butter, one pillow, a loaf of bread, two tin cups, a change of clothes for each of them, a brush, and a bar of soap.

"Porker, thank you so much for doing this for us."

He smiled and his cheeks turned bright red under the praise.

"That's what friends do. We are friends, right?"

"Oh yes, of course we are. Do you want to eat with us?"

"Nope. That's all for you. I have one more thing too, I'll be right back."

He ran out before she could say anything else.

Loralye and Isaiah ate together, thankful for the nourishment after a hard day of work. Loralye's muscles ached from the pressure she had to use to get the dirt off the walls. She tried to push the image from her thoughts of the blood she had seen going down one of them. She had done her best to clean it before Isaiah saw it, and she hoped she had protected him from the sight.

"Why are you crying," Isaiah said.

Not realizing that she had been, she quickly pulled herself together.

"I'm really tired. I think the day has just gotten to me."

"I'm tired too. I keep thinking about Mara and Tim; all of them really. Do you think they are okay Miss Loralye?"

"I hope so Isaiah, I hope so."

They sat together in the room, both caught up in their own thoughts of the children whom they had been with just hours before. How quickly circumstances could change.

Porker arrived winded sometime later. Loralye had forgotten that he had something else for them. He came empty-handed and Loralye was confused.

"Now, before I bring this in here, I just want to tell you how hard I worked for it. I have this buddy up top who helps me out. Well, we help each other. I get him what he wants, and he gets me things I want."

"He was part of your delivery. He told me one of his people left something up top, and I asked him for it. Took me forever to get back up there. I hate all those stairs."

He went back into the hall and brought in the small carpet bag Loralye had left days ago.

She ran to Porker and wrapped her arms around him, not even caring about the bodily stench he carried. She hugged him as if he were her brother. She didn't care about the dampness of his sweaty skin and didn't notice the tears that were falling freely down his face.

"I'm glad you like it," he said gruffly, doing his best to overcome his emotions.

Embarrassed by his tears, he let go of Loralye and walked towards the door.

"I'll be back to get you both in the morning."

He went quietly out of the small room, locking the door behind him.

Loralye bent down and took her bag into her arms. Sitting on the small bed, she opened it.

"What's in there Miss Loralye," Isaiah asked, knowing that whatever it was, it was very special.

Loralye reached in, took her wedding photo out, and unwrapped it. The glass had cracked somewhere during the bag's trip from home. She ran her hand over the jagged glass, smiling at the picture of her husband that she thought she would never see again.

"Have you ever done a puzzle before and lost one of the pieces? This is a little piece of home Isaiah; a piece I thought I would never see again."

"Is that man your husband?"

"He sure was."

"What happened to him?"

Loralye closed her eyes. Unashamed, she allowed every tear to fall that wanted to.

"He died a hero, Isaiah, saving a young boy."

Isaiah smiled and took Loralye by the hand.

"That's real special that you get to do that together."

Loralye held his hand, and reluctantly she opened her eyes and asked, "Do what together?"

"You both are saving people Loralye." Closing her eyes tight, she pulled Isaiah into a warm embrace. Her lip began to quiver as God opened her eyes to that revelation. She was still doing things with her Abe, and even as he had given his last breath to help another, God was putting her on a path to do the same.

"You're right Isaiah, we both get to help children, don't we?"

He hugged her tightly. "I'm glad that you're helping me."

"Me too," she said, and she meant it. God had yoked her with her husband, and to her surprise, had called them both to the same calling. By helping the children, she could continue the legacy that Abe had started. The legacy of saving the children.

Chapter Nineteen

New York, New York, Present Day

Three weeks later, Kay was on her way to meet Miss Craig, her childhood teacher. She did her best to calm her nerves. She prayed that the Lord would be with her, and that she wouldn't show anger or rage to the woman who had changed her life forever, many years ago.

Carter sat beside her, his hand holding hers in the back of their car. Al, their driver and protector, drove them to a little restaurant a few hours away.

"Maybe this isn't such a good idea Carter, maybe she is setting us up."

"Kay, this is the right move. We prayed about it, remember? We both felt at peace on this meeting."

"I know we did but now I'm not so sure. What if something happens to Hope while we are gone?"

"Hope is in the best of hands. You know your brother wouldn't allow anyone to come near her. Plus, we left our other guard there."

She took a deep breath.

"Carter, what if I can't control my anger towards this woman who ruined my life, and was a part of all of those children dying in The Imaginarium?"

He reached up to Kay's face and gently pulled her towards him. Looking into her eyes, he said what was in his heart.

"Kay, I know what happened to you as a child was horrific. You have seen and experienced things that no one should ever have to endure. But have you ever thought of what would have happened if you hadn't been kidnapped? Or, if you hadn't been taken to The Imaginarium?"

"Just think of all that you have accomplished. You most likely wouldn't have gone into the service, wouldn't have been the mayor, and you probably wouldn't have met me either."

He winked at her playfully and brought her in for a hug.

"Not to mention all the children that you have saved so far. I know that your past was hurtful and a mess, but look at the glory God has brought out of it."

She leaned back into him, knowing he was right. She felt the same way as well, though it was hard not to imagine what it would have been like growing up with a normal past, with a normal family.

"Pray that I can be strong today, Carter. Pray I don't ruin this chance with Miss Craig."

"I haven't stopped. Remember Exodus 14:14, 'The Lord will fight for you, you need only to hold your peace.'"

"Who would have ever thought that holding your peace would seem like such an impossible task."

"Isn't that the truth? I felt like I was going to fail last week when they didn't take our trash cans. Man, that gets under my skin."

She chuckled, knowing he was trying to cheer her up.

"I love you. Thank you for coming with me.

"There isn't anywhere else I would rather be."

They sat and watched the scenery together as they drew closer to their destination. Half an hour later, Al pulled into the small restaurant and parked the car. He went in first to make sure it was safe, before leading the couple inside. There at the back table, sat a woman, alone.

"That's her," Kay whispered.

"How do you know?" Carter asked.

"She's missing a finger."

Kay left Carter's side and walked up to the table.

"Miss Craig, is that you?" Kay asked.

The woman stood up so quickly, that she hit her head on the light that was hanging a tad too low over the corner table. She rubbed the spot on her temple as she moved closer to Kay to greet her.

"Lailey, you are just beautiful. Seeing you on television all of these years, I knew that you had grown into a lovely woman. I can recognize a hint of the little girl that used to sit and listen to me tell stories all those years ago."

"Thank you for taking the time to meet with me, Miss Craig. I hope that this is going to be beneficial for all of us, especially the children."

"Please call me Andrea. I haven't been called Miss Craig in years. I hope that you believe me when I say that I truly am sorry for the part that I played in all of this. My life has been in a downward spiral ever since that dreaded day."

"I forgive you," Kay said before she realized what she was saying. The words surprised her; they were so easy to say. The moment she had been dreading for the last few weeks was over within the first two minutes of their meeting. She felt as if a weight had been lifted off her, and her next breath was the easiest one she had ever inhaled.

"Thank you. I know I don't deserve that."

The older woman sat back down in the chair closest to the wall that she had vacated moments before. Kay sat opposite her and waved Carter over.

"Do you mind if my husband joins us, Andrea? He is helping me catch the bad guys, so to speak."

"Absolutely. I love seeing how he is always right beside you, or close by at the conferences that are broadcast. His support for you is so heart warming."

Carter sat down beside Kay and held his hand out to Andrea.

"It's a pleasure to meet you, mam, I'm Carter."

Andrea awkwardly held out her left hand and wrapped her fingers around Carter's.

"Carter, it is a pleasure to meet you as well. Sorry, my other hand has seen better days."

"Oh of course," Carter said, a little embarrassed that he hadn't thought to use his opposite hand for their greeting. Just then, the waitress came and the awkward moment passed.

The young girl wore her dark brunette hair in two pigtails that almost reached her shoulders. The uniform of the small diner was a white and red candy-striped button-down shirt tucked into whitewashed jeans. Her mouth didn't stop chewing on a piece of gum when she asked with a thick Southern accent, "What can I get for ya?"

"Order whatever you like Andrea, it's on us."

She smiled and said, "I will take a coke and the fish and chips special I saw on the board up front dear."

The girl, Cindy, if her name tag was correct, nodded her head as she asked, "Is the slaw ok with that?"

"Oh, that would be perfect, thank you."

"And for the two of you?"

They both ordered the fish and chips as well. Kay switched the coke out for a diet and Carter ordered a root beer float.

"I wish all my tables were this easy. I'll be right back with your drinks." With that, she headed towards the kitchen.

"I don't plan to waste your time. I hope that I can be of service to the capture of this evil organization. When I was approached by the man all those years ago, to get my mother into the medical trial, he didn't share very much information with me."

Kay's thoughts began to run a million miles a minute. She wondered if this was a complete waste of time. How was Andrea going to be able to help them at all? As the heat began to rush to her face in anger, Carter grabbed her hand under the table. His touch was like a cooling balm that started at her head and worked its way into her soul, and she was glad when he took the lead.

"Anything that you can help us with Andrea, will be greatly appreciated. We have had some success, but we keep hitting dead ends, or we will find a few children, and the tunnel we expose will be caved in. Then it takes us months to get anywhere."

Cindy came with their drinks. "If I can get you anything else, just give me a holler. Your fish and chips should be up in 10-15 minutes."

"Thank you," Andrea said, placing a straw in her drink. She took a long sip, her good hand gripping the glass, she closed her eyes in appreciation of the cold drink.

"Coke is just not the same overseas. This tastes delightful." She took a deep breath. "Thank you, Carter, for sharing that. I can't imagine how heart-wrenching it must be to be so close and then have a few months stall every time you're getting somewhere."

"You got that right; it feels impossible sometimes."

She took another sip of her drink, then moved it to the side. Leaning in, she asked in a subdued voice, "Does the name Shawn

Williams mean anything to you?" Carter looked at Kay before they both leaned in closer to the woman sitting across the table.

Andrea continued, "I had to do some digging before I found it."

"Found what?"

"The name. When my mother died, I decided that I was going to tell my story, so I began to do some research. I wanted, not only to pay for what I had done, but I wanted the real men behind this evil to be brought to justice.

"When I thought I had enough information to take to the States, I packed a bag and bought the first flight home I could find. The day my flight was going to leave was the same day I was attacked. When I woke up in the hospital, I had the feeling that someone was still watching me, that I wasn't alone.

"I don't know how it was possible, but I knew that I should pretend to be asleep, even though I had been out like a light for who knows how long. I barely opened one of my eyes and tried to get a feel for where I was. The rhythmic sound of the heart rate monitor, the IV that was in my arm, and the bright tile all pointed to being at a hospital.

"Just as I began to call out for someone, to let them know I was awake, I saw a man in the doorway. I didn't have any friends, so I knew that he couldn't be there out of concern. He was looking at a newspaper and was distracted. I felt for my call light and was more than thankful when I realized it was in my good hand. They must have known I would wake up at some point and would need help.

"I pressed the button and continued to pretend to be asleep. When the nurse came in, the man was gone."

"Was that Shawn Williams?" Kay asked. She was held completely captive by the story that was being told.

"No, he wasn't. I couldn't sleep that night, afraid that the man might come back to finish what he started. I was able to walk around in my room, my missing finger, blood loss, and a slight concussion were my only injuries. That night, I sat in the only chair in my room and noticed a piece of paper stuffed down into the side of the chair."

Carter and Kay were shoulder to shoulder, ready to hear what was on the mysterious note.

"Did it have his name on it? Was that him? Do you remember what it said?"

Andrea simply sat back into her chair, took her purse in hand, unzipped the inside pocket, and pulled out a crumbled-up piece of paper.

Chapter Twenty

A ndrea handed the weathered piece of paper to Carter. He and Kay smoothed it out on the table in front of them, searching the text for the answers they had been looking for. Shawn Williams was written in bold, capital letters, in the middle of the paper. A series of numbers were scribbled everywhere, surrounding the name in what seemed to be a rhythmic pattern.

Before they could ask what it all meant, Cindy came from the kitchen with their order in hand. Strategically she carried the three plates without a tray, placing an order of Fish 'n Chips in front of each of them. She took extra dressing containers, filled with tartar sauce out of her apron. "Can I get y'all anything else?"

"This is perfect, thank you, Cindy," Andrea said, while opening the little black plastic cup of tartar sauce with her fully fingered hand. The girl left and headed back to the kitchen, yelling something about another order to the line cook.

Kay waited for Andrea to say something, to say anything, about the paper she had just shared, but she simply sat across the table and continued to work on her meal. Taking her butter knife, she spread the tartar sauce on the crispy fish. Andrea looked up, surprised that the couple was watching her so intently.

"I'm so sorry, I haven't eaten since breakfast yesterday. The note mystified me as well when I first saw it. Who knew a group of numbers could be so intriguing."

Kay apologized for rushing her and encouraged the frail woman to eat before going into further detail. Carter took the opportunity to eat his meal as well, stating that he hadn't eaten in at least two hours either.

They laughed and made idle chit-chat while they ate the best basket of Fish 'n Chips that any of them had eaten in quite a while. Kay could only manage a few bites because her nerves were as wound up as a knot of necklaces tangled together. Carter finished his food and then helped Kay with her fries.

When Andrea had eaten as much as she could, she pulled a notebook out of her purse.

"Now, back to the note. When I first saw it, I couldn't make heads or tails of the thing. After I was released from the hospital, I lay low for quite a while. You can imagine the fear that I had to overcome, after being attacked in the way that I had been.

"I was all alone now that mother had passed, and all of my friends and relatives believed that I had been killed in the school shooting. It took me a few years to start trying to put the pieces together."

Carter nodded his head, understanding how frightening it must have been for the woman. He himself had felt that same fear trying to rise every day in his concern for Kay. Even now, fear began to creep in at that very moment. Carter looked over at Al and saw that the man was watching as closely as ever. He relaxed a little and leaned back in his seat and asked if she had ever been able to make any sense of the note. Andrea opened her notebook and handed that across the table as well.

"I believe that I have. It took a lot of digging and a lot of stones thrown without hitting anything, but finally one day, I made a connection. It all lines up, and if this isn't the actual meaning, I will be very surprised."

Kay and Carter looked at her notes, looked at each other, and back down again. Kay couldn't believe her eyes. She was dumbfounded that the little woman was able figure out such a mess of letters and numbers.

"You're a decoder, Andrea! This is mind-blowing. How did you ever figure this out?"

"I bought a burner phone a few years after the accident. I would go from coffee shop to coffee shop, connecting to different internet servers every few days. I tried to find any connection I could between the name and the numbers. It took me four years to connect everything. The first one was the hardest. After that though, there was a pattern to follow.

"I wanted to bring this back to the States sooner, but as I have told you, the fear was crippling. Now that I am running out of time, I just don't really care what happens to me. It's time the truth comes out. Whatever that means for me, I'm ready to accept it.

"I want you two to take this and do what you can with it. I will help in any other way that I can, but this is my golden ticket, so to speak. This is all I've got."

"This is perfect. Thank you so much, Andrea. I think this is exactly what we have been praying for."

Andrea smiled at the girl-turned-woman that sat across from her. A tear slid down her cheek and she let it stay. Kay thought at that moment, that the woman looked as if she had just found peace.

"I wrote my number and where I'm staying in the back of that book. Don't hesitate to call if you have any questions about what's in there. I wrote it out in as much detail as I could. I think, however, I better get back to my room. I'm trying not to spend too much time out and about."

"Can we drive you back to your hotel?" Carter asked, standing to help her out of her chair.

"Oh no. I would not dream of inconveniencing you like that. I'll be fine. You two get to work, and I will be praying."

She grabbed her bag and smiled one last time at Kay, looking at her for an exceptionally long time. Kay wondered if she was imagining her as a little girl, eager to play Little Red Riding Hood all those years ago in her classroom.

"Thank you for lunch. Goodbye now," she said, waving her good hand. They watched her leave the restaurant and continued watching her through the glass windows until she was no longer in sight.

"I think we should get going as well, Kay," Carter said as he held tight to the note and notebook they had just been given. He tapped them and said, "We have some digging to do."

Kay left a $100 bill on the table, and they headed back out to the car, Al leading the way. As they left the small town and worked their way back to the big city, they looked over the pages of notes that Andrea had given them. Each one explained every number that was on the page with the words Shawn Williams in the center.

"How did she ever figure this out? It's like a puzzle. It baffles me that she was able to make these connections."

Kay now admired the woman in more ways than she could say. The woman who had destroyed her life years ago had now connected the pieces she had been searching for her entire adult life.

Carter looked at the notes on the first page.

"See here babe? This is where she found that first connection she was talking about."

Kay looked at Andrea's notes. She could see the excitement in the woman's handwriting as her normally neat script got smaller and smaller.

He read it aloud. "I have googled Shawn Williams hundreds of times. How did I not catch this beforehand? Every website is a series of numbers. If I connect each series of numbers in an alphabetical sequence following the website series of numbers, we have names."

Kay sat up excitedly. "I'm telling you, Carter! She is brilliant!"

"I know! I don't think I would have ever figured this out. Look at this one, 089753832-098345, that's Sanfranmillerdistrict. Here, look at what she wrote. San Francisco Miller District is a possible tunnel entry. There are locations, people's names, everything. Kay, there are hundreds of different paths we can take with this!"

Kay and Carter looked at every single journal entry. The hours spent on each one was impressive. After Andrea had decoded each number, she then researched every person and location that she had uncovered.

When they reached home, Al walked them in. Saul was at the house with baby Hope sleeping soundly in his arms, while his wife did the dishes in the kitchen.

"Thank you, Saul," Kay said, "for taking time off work to watch the baby. It means a lot."

"No problem at all sis. I'm glad to do it. She is the sweetest little thing. She sat with me almost the whole time. Kailey has been making her smile, tickling her tiny feet."

He handed the baby to her gently, smiling at the sister he was still getting to know. "Did you guys figure anything out? Get any answers?"

Carter looked over at Kay before smiling from ear to ear.

"I think it's safe to say, we might finally have the lead we have been looking for."

Chapter Twenty-One

December 24th, 1963

The days began to meld together as Loralye and Isaiah worked tirelessly, cleaning the empty rooms. Every day, Porker would come and let them out of their room, give them their assignments for the day, and leave them to get it done.

Loralye tried to find a way out some days. On other days, when she was too tired to think, she robotically scrubbed the walls and floors of the dank, cold tombs she wished she had never seen.

Isaiah was always checking doors, praying that God would leave one unlocked for them. They never were. The doors were always locked tight, except for the ones that weren't being used, the ones that needed cleaning, the infirmary, and the supply closet.

Today was harder than normal for Loralye. They had been given four rooms to clean, two more than normal. Her stomach was growing by the day. The tight protruding bump seemed to have a life of its own as the babe within went from one side to another. The round mass made it hard for her to bend down and scrub.

She was thankful for the unlikely friend she and Isaiah had found in Porker. Daily, he brought them food, fresh water, and 'décor' for their small dwelling. She smiled to herself as she remembered the little toy cat, he had brought for the baby the night before.

Loralye paused, as she scrubbed the floor of the last room they had to clean for the day. It was a large room that looked as if a bloody massacre had happened only moments before. She took in a few slow breaths, then continued to use what little strength she had left to work the grime off the ground.

A few minutes later, she had to pause again, the tightness in her stomach causing her to lose her breath.

"Are you okay Miss Loralye," Isaiah asked, concern lacing his voice. He stooped next to her, holding on to her elbow for support as she got off the floor and back on her feet.

"I will be fine Isaiah. I think that I'm working a little harder than this child would like me to be."

He led her over to the bed, glad that they had cleaned the mattresses first.

"You sit down and rest. I can finish this."

Loralye protested, trying weakly to fight the offer of the young boy.

"I couldn't have you finish this all alone young man. I'm capable of helping until we are done."

"Please Loralye, let me do it. This is the last room we have to do today. I know I can get it done real quick if you would just give me a chance. It might not look as good as when you do it, but I'll try real hard, I promise."

She couldn't help but let him do it. Not because she wanted to rest, but because of the heart he had that shone so brightly. The little boy had proved repeatedly that he was a true servant. Not the kind that served the upper class, but the kind that followed the example of Jesus. The kind that served behind closed doors when no one else was watching.

"If you insist, I will gratefully take you up on it. Thank you, Isaiah, you are a Godsend."

He stood up straighter, smiled, and got to work right where Loralye had left off. After the room was finished, they headed back to their room for the night. Loralye paused every few feet, breathing faster, unable to catch her breath.

Isaiah worried about his friend and surrogate mother. He stopped every time she did, waiting patiently for her to continue down the tunnel that never seemed to end.

"What's wrong Miss Loralye? Do you need to see a doctor?"

"No, no I'm all right Isaiah. I believe that it might be time for the baby to make its way into the world."

Isaiah smiled and jumped up and down.

"Do you mean it Miss Loralye? Tonight, the baby might come?"

"I think it just might. I've been trying to keep track of how often the pains come. I wish I had a watch. Every few steps though, it is most assuredly getting closer."

"I always wanted to have a baby brother. Do you think maybe it's a boy? Not that if it is a boy, he would be my brother, but I would like to think of him that way if it's all right with you."

Tears welled in her eyes as she looked at the little pale-skinned boy who had become her closest friend. She wondered how people could be so different. There were some who hated the color of her skin so much, that they had killed her Abe because of it, and now, she would never see him again until the day of glory.

Then there were others, like Isaiah, who wanted to call her child his brother. She wished that more people were like him.

"I would be honored for the baby to be your brother or sister Isaiah. You will make a fine big brother."

He smiled, took Loralye's hand, and continued to walk with her back to their room. They paused several times as she worked through every contraction, each seeming to last a little longer than the one before it.

When they made it back to their room, he helped Loralye into bed, lifting each leg as gently as he could. Isaiah removed her shoes and covered her with a blanket.

"What else can I do to help? Should I ask Porker to get a doctor?"

"I'm afraid we aren't going to have a doctor's help this time. I may need you to help me bring this child into the world, Isaiah. Is that something you think you can do?"

"I think that if you need my help, God will help me do it. I don't know nothing about this though, so you're going to have to tell me what to do."

Loralye tried not to let fear cripple her. She herself had only ever seen one baby born and she was just a child then. Not wanting to scare poor Isaiah more than he already was, she decided she was going to have to act like she knew exactly what she was doing.

"We are going to need Porker to get us a few things. Do you think you can go down the hall and find him for me?"

"Yes, I can. He should be in that room they eat and play cards in, right?"

"I would think so, yes. Just tell him when he has time, I would like to have a word with him about tomorrow."

"Okay, I'll go right now. I'll be back as soon as I can."

"Be careful Isaiah."

"I will be." He hurriedly left the room, understanding that he was the only help that Loralye had.

Isaiah came back alone, and Loralye prayed that Porker wouldn't be far behind. Her contractions were coming even closer together now and the pain was almost unbearable. Isaiah stood by the bed, holding on to her hand, squeezing just as tightly as she was.

"I don't like this, Miss Loralye. I can't make you feel better. I can't help."

She fell back against her pillow, the last contraction taking her breath away. Why hadn't she thought to have Porker bring her the items she needed before she was in the midst of giving birth? She couldn't wait any longer.

She thought about what she needed. Rags and hot water? Scissors? String to tie off the umbilical cord? She wasn't even sure what items to ask for. "Oh Lord, I need Your help now more than ever," she said louder than she intended to.

Looking over at her labor partner, she could see the fear in his eyes. She had to say something to calm his nerves. There was no sense in both of them being worried to death.

"You are helping Isaiah. Now before the pains come back, I need you to do something for me. Go get our work pad of paper and a pencil."

He ran to do her bidding, thankful for a task he could accomplish.

"Not again!" Loralye screamed, as another contraction came fast and hard. She worked to control her breathing, but it was no use. She couldn't blow in and out in a steady rhythm when she thought that she might die right then and there. She panted heavily, doing her best not to scream again. She waited for the contraction to ease, but it felt as if it would never end.

As it finally let up, they both heard a pop as water began to come out of her in a steady gush. The liquid seeped into her mattress and began to drip out of the bottom onto the concrete floor. Isaiah knelt to get a better look under the bed.

"That's ok Miss Loralye. No one would blame you for not making it to the toilet if they were in as much pain as you are. I'll clean it up, don't worry."

Loralye, thankful that she was in-between contractions, smiled at the boy. Oh, how she wished he didn't have to be the one to help her.

"Isaiah, that was my water breaking. It won't be long now before this child takes his first breath out here in the open.

"Now, I'm going to write down a list of items I need. You're going to have to go back to Porker. I'm sorry. I was hoping we had a little more time."

As if the man-child knew that his name had been said, Porker came through the threshold without knocking.

"What do you need Loralye? Isaiah looked as nervous as a racehorse about to take his first run on the track when he said you needed me."

Porker locked eyes with Loralye and knew exactly what was happening.

"By golly why didn't you say so kid? I'll go get the kit."

Loralye tried to stop him, needing to tell him what she would need for the baby, but another contraction came just as he left the room. She moaned through the force that was slowly pushing the baby down her birth canal. All her thoughts left her as she tried to relax through the intense pain that wouldn't let go of her.

Isaiah got a wet rag and patted the moisture off her forehead. "I don't know much about this Miss, but I think you're doing a real fine job."

She grabbed Isaiah's hand and brought it to her lips. She kissed it and told him that he was doing an excellent job too.

Porker came back into the room carrying a tote of some sort filled with medical instruments. Right behind him came another man that she had never seen. The tall, wiry man was void of emotion. There was absolutely no expression on his face to indicate his thoughts.

His thin white skin almost matched the white stringy hair that graced part of his head. Wasting no time, he walked over to the bed and threw the blanket off her. Another contraction hit just as he scooted Loralye down to the end of the bed.

Impatient, he didn't wait for the pain to subside before he did an examination of her. Isaiah quickly turned his head when he realized what was going on. He threw his hands over his ears as Loralye cried out in pain at both the roughness of the man and the contraction.

"Are we letting this one live Porker," the man asked, looking away from the bed and towards the man who was pacing the floor as if it were his baby about to be born.

"Of course, were keeping it Doc. What's wrong with you!" Porker exclaimed gesturing angrily with his arms, shocked that the man would even ask such a question.

Loralye's heart pounded in her chest. It had never crossed her mind that they might choose to kill her baby. Take it, maybe. But kill it? Take its life before it even began?

Panic began to set in at the realization of the absolute power they had over her. She had lost her Abe, and now the reality that she might lose her baby started to sink in.

The Doc shrugged his shoulders and turned back towards Loralye.

"I just thought I'd ask Porker. I'm not used to the ones giving birth being so old. Get me that chair boy," he yelled at Isaiah who quickly did as he was asked.

As if on cue, another contraction hit her again. Loralye sat up as the pain took on a life of its own. Isaiah rushed to her side, grabbing ahold of her hand. She took it, thankful for the lifeline that it offered. Porker surprised her by coming to the other side of the bed and taking her other hand.

Without being told what she needed to do, Loralye's body took over and began to push the baby out. She bore down, giving everything, she had left to give, her body completely exhausted. The contraction ended and she fell back against the bed.

"I can see the top of the head now woman. Looks to be larger than what I'm used to seeing down here. You're going to have to work harder to get it out. During the next contraction, give it everything you've got."

Doubt was all that Loralye felt. Never once had anyone told her how hard the pains were, how messy and excruciating it was to bring new life into the world. Another pain came and she quickly asked for the Lord to give her strength.

Loralye got back into position, leaning forward, holding on to the two boys on either side of her. She screamed as the baby squirmed its way into the world for the first time.

Doc caught the child in surprise. "This is the biggest baby I have ever seen!" He said, astounded at the sheer mass that wiggled in his arms.

He handed the child to Loralye, her body now completely spent. She held it to her chest, staring at it in wonder.

Isaiah smiled with tears in his eyes. "You did it, Miss Loralye, you got him out!"

"Him? It's a boy?" She said excitedly, realizing that she hadn't even looked when Doc had handed the baby to her.

"It's a boy!" Pork wailed, crying in relief that Loralye had the baby, and both were alive and well.

Doc stood up, went over to the bucket of water, and washed his hands. He told Porker to snap out of it and act like a man before he headed out of the room.

"I will be back in twenty minutes to cut the cord."

Loralye thought that she saw a smile on the old man's face as he left the foursome, but she couldn't be sure.

"I seen birth lots of times Loralye, but I ain't never been a part of it. He sure is big ain't he?" Porker didn't try to hide the tear that was sliding down his cheek.

She took in the size of the baby in her arms. He was longer than her forearm and as dark as night. He began to cry, and the noise was music to her ears. Her boy was alive and well. Tears wet her cheeks too, she couldn't help but marvel at the miracle that had just taken place.

"What are you going to call him Miss Loralye?" Isaiah asked, not taking his eyes off the baby.

Loralye smiled down at her son, as he grasped her finger with his hand. His little fingers wrapped around her finger and squeezed. She thought of Abe and how happy he would have been in that moment. Tears continued to fall as she mourned the thought of him never meeting the son he had always wanted.

Taking a deep breath, she said, "His name is Abe after his father."

"I like that name Loralye; I like it a lot."

"I do too. We will call him Brew for short though. His father loved him a dark cup of coffee every morning. His skin is that same color as those dark beans he liked so well."

"Brew fits him, don't it?" Porker said, smiling down at the little one who had been the first born out of desire and love down in The Hollow. Yes, Brew was a miracle indeed.

Chapter Twenty-Two

Loralye watched as Brew slept soundly in her arms. She was thankful that he only knew peace and comfort at this point in his life. He was unaware of the dungeon they were in, at the loss they had experienced.

She looked over at the only chair in the room and smiled at Porker, who had somehow managed to fall asleep sitting up. His mouth hung open, a loud snore escaping him every few breaths. Little Isaiah slept at her feet, giving her as much room as his body could. He had wanted to sleep on the floor, but she wouldn't have it.

The baby was a fierce nurser and woke every few hours to suckle on his mother. She decided that birth and motherhood were sacred. She was in awe that her body had everything the small bundle in her arms needed for survival. She knew that she would need to come up with a plan to keep the baby with her for as long as possible.

When Porker woke up the next day, he quickly left the room to get something for the three of them to eat. Gone for the better part of an hour, Loralye and Isaiah were surprised when he came back into the room with a tray holding three delicious-looking plated breakfasts.

He placed the tray on the side of the bed, proud of what he had provided.

"Merry Christmas! See there? I put red and green food coloring in the batter." He pointed to the food excitedly, taking one of the three plates from the tray. He walked happily back to his chair and began to eat the flapjacks he had made.

Loralye laughed when he poked the top sphere with his fork and brought it to his mouth in one big bite. He couldn't even close his lips together until he had managed to wiggle some of the dough down into his throat.

Isaiah handed her a plate before taking his own. The sweet, syrup-coated pancakes tasted like heaven. Loralye didn't realize how hungry she had been. When was the last time she had had something to eat? It must have been breakfast the day before she decided.

Isaiah ate two of his pancakes and then slid the third onto Loralye's plate.

"Isaiah, you get that pancake back on your plate right this minute."

"I want you to have it, Loralye. Please don't make me take it back, it's Christmas and I don't have nothing else for you and the baby."

She smiled at him as she cut the pancake in half.

"How about we split it? See, I haven't anything for you either. I lost track of the days too. I thought we were still a few days away from Christmas."

He said that was a great gift and accepted half of the pancake as she slid it back onto his plate. Porker had also brought them each a small, wrapped gift. Loralye was surprised to see that he had thought to get them something.

"I know you don't got nothing for me, and that's ok. I have connections to things on the outside. That's how I can do things like this you know."

He looked very smug, wanting to impress them with his connections with the outside world.

Isaiah opened his first. He squealed with delight when a shiny red yoyo fell out of its little box.

"Thank you, Porker!" He ran over and hugged the man for the second time, and Porker awkwardly patted him on the back.

"You're welcome, Isaiah. I used to have one just like it from my Pappy a long time ago. Now you go on and open yours Loralye. I hope you like it!"

"I'm sure I will Porker, thank you for thinking of us like this."

She used her free hand to open up the package that was wrapped in old newspapers, as her other arm caressed her sleeping babe. When she removed the last of the paper, she held in her hand a small, navy-colored book. Flipping it over to see the front, she read on the cover '*New Testament, Psalms and Proverbs*'. She looked at him in surprise.

"I know it's nothing as exciten as a new toy, but I hear you singing those songs about God and talking about scriptures and things. I thought you might like to read more about that church stuff." He looked unsure of his choice, wondering if maybe Loralye would have liked a yoyo like Isaiah, or maybe a slinky instead.

Loralye handed the baby over to Isaiah, then carefully got out of bed. Still sore, she took her time walking over to where Porker sat.

"You couldn't have brought me a better gift in all the world dear friend, and I thank you for it from the bottom of my heart."

She hugged him tightly, imagining what kind of man he could have been if only he had been brought up right.

They spent the day watching Isaiah play with his yoyo and laughing at the stories Porker told of how he adventured to get the gifts from the great outside. As the day continued, Loralye read the story of another birth that changed history forever. She read the story of Jesus.

Isaiah and Porker listened earnestly. Loralye did her best to keep the story engaging, doing different voices, and asking them questions as she went along. Porker surprised her. He was just as interested in the little book as Isaiah was.

When she had finished the story of Jesus' birth, they asked her to continue to read. She read a few more chapters, ending with the story of the good Samaritan.

"I'm afraid that's all I can get through tonight. I can barely keep my eyes open." She closed the book, and held on to it, not wanting to set it down.

Porker stood up, supposing he should go and let her rest.

"Do you really think all those things are true Loralye," he asked, as he walked towards the door.

"With all my heart Porker. With all my heart."

"Maybe I could hear some more about Him tomorrow?"

"I would like that very much. We can continue right where we left off if you'd like."

"That'll be great! I'll see if we have any cookies left and bring those too. There is nothing like some cookies and a good story. Merry Christmas!" he said, as he closed the door and locked it from the outside.

Isaiah headed back toward the end of the bed, just as tired as she was. He cuddled up against Loralye's feet just as the lights went out. "He's pretty amazing, isn't He?" Isaiah said, half asleep already.

"Porker has been a bigger blessing than I ever thought possible."

Isaiah chuckled. Letting out another yawn he said, "I don't mean Porker, I mean Jesus. He is pretty amazing."

"Oh yes, He is. Just wait until we read more about Him."

"I can't wait. I really do hope Porker brings cookies tomorrow night too."

"Oh, me too Isaiah, me too. Merry Christmas."

"Merry Christmas Loralye."

As Loralye lay there with her new baby sleeping in her arms, and the Bible in her hands, she decided it really had been a Merry Christmas after all.

Chapter Twenty-Three

January 1ˢᵗ, 1964

Porker came in early that morning to give Loralye and Isaiah their assigned rooms to clean for the day.

"I hate making you get back to work, but I don't think I can make Toby wait any longer. I'm surprised that he has let you wait this long already."

"That's okay Porker, I'm thankful for the time you have managed to get me."

"How are you going to work with the baby," he asked, worried about how she would manage.

"I made this out of one of the sheets you brought me." She proceeded to lift baby Brew off the bed, she then placed him tightly against her. Then, wrapped the sheet around her body, fitting him carefully inside the folds, she left his face exposed to the outside, all the while keeping him snug as rug. She walked from one end of the room to the other, showing Porker how easy it was to walk with him nestled close, while her hands remained free.

"Well, I'll be! That might just be the brightest idea I ever seen."

She smiled at Isaiah. The contraption had been his brilliant idea. Loralye couldn't help but brag on his genius.

"Isaiah had the idea all on his own. I think that women everywhere would benefit from having two hands free, to get things done while carrying around a new baby."

"Good job Isaiah," Porker said hesitantly. "I see my brain is rubbin' off on you. Looks like we both come up with some promising ideas, Huh?" Porker's shoulder slouched, his hurt of not producing a solution for baby Brew himself, evident.

"Oh yeah, Porker it has," Isaiah said enthusiastically, sensing that his friend needed encouragement too. "If you hadn't brought the sheets, we wouldn't have had nothing to make the baby holder with, and I probably would never have come up with the idea."

Porker straightened up, a look of pride on his face. "You know, you're right about that Isaiah. When I grabbed those sheets, I did have the baby in mind."

He knelt down to get eye-to-eye with his little friend. "You and I are like this," he said, moving his two fingers from in front of his eyes, to Isaiah's.

Isaiah laughed, took his yoyo out of his pocket, and began to work on his latest trick. Loralye smiled as she followed the two out of the room and towards their first job of the day. She prayed that God would give her the strength she needed to get the work done that was at hand. Her body was still recovering from delivering her baby just the week before.

Porker brought them to their first room to clean, letting them know he would return in a few hours. He left them to go inside alone. Loralye walked in first, wanting to inspect the room to see what materials they would need from the supply closet. She was telling Isaiah about how nice it was to walk around a bit before she saw it. Closing the door quickly, she kept Isaiah from going inside.

"What is it, Miss Loralye?"

Loralye tried to keep the bile down in her stomach, the desire for it to escape her almost out of her control. Trying to keep it together for his sake, she smiled before saying, "We know what we need. Why don't you go get the bucket of hot water with bleach, several rags, and the new mop Porker told us about? I'm going to wait here and feed the baby."

"Okay, I'll go, if you're sure. I will be back Loralye, don't start without me." Isaiah took off towards the supply closet, running as fast as his legs could take him.

Loralye rushed back into the room, moving as quickly as she could. She knew she only had a few minutes before Isaiah would be back. Loralye couldn't understand how any of this was possible, how anyone could treat another human being this way.

She prayed to God for help as she neared the small lifeless body that was lying face down on the floor. Carefully, she turned the little brunette over. She took the lifeless hands and crossed the child's arms over her chest. Dried blood stained the little girls uniform in a dozen various places.

Wiping the tears away, Loralye adjusted Abe and then dragged the little girl towards the infirmary by her ankles. She prayed for the remaining children down in the tunnel, for Isaiah, and for Brew. The stiff body was small. She couldn't have been more than six years old. She hated that she wasn't able to carry the poor little one, whose life never had a chance to get started, but her body was too weak.

The girl had burns of some sort on her arms, bruises on her bare legs, and dried blood on the side of her mouth. Loralye wished that she could hold her close, that she could have helped her in some way. She laid her next to the large incinerator, unwilling to place the body in the burning oven herself.

She cried out to God. "Where are You? Don't You see these hurting children? Don't You see how they are being treated here? When are You going to do something about it? Where are You!"

She raced to get back to the room, wanting to be there when Isaiah returned. She made it just in time and could see him concentrating on not spilling the bucket of water he was dragging down the tunnel. Going to meet him, she helped him get the bucket of warm bleach water into the room.

Isaiah got right to work, not noticing the despair on Loralye's face. Isaiah talked without pause about the baby, about Christmas, the cookies they had gotten, his red yoyo, and the stories Loralye had been reading to them from the Bible.

Loralye tried to be genuine, answering the questions he had about the Word, and about Jesus. She tried to keep the bitterness out of her heart, realizing the threat to her child becoming increasingly more of a possibility each day.

The what ifs began to creep in. What if they never got out of this place? What if they took her child and never brought him back? What if she died, and there was no one else to take care of Brew and Isaiah?

She didn't notice when Toby came in until his shoes came into view on the floor she had been scrubbing.

"Loralye, when you're done here, I want to have a word with you in my office," he said, leaving before she answered.

After a moment of silence, Isaiah spoke out the question she had been thinking.

"What do you think he wants Miss Loralye? Do you think he's going to take Brew from us?"

Loralye looked up at Isaiah, his bottom lip quivering with emotion. Angry that she always had to be the strong one, that she had to be the one to keep the brave face, Loralye tried to keep the bitterness and fear out of her reply.

"I'm sure he isn't going to take our Brew Isaiah, what would he want with a baby?"

"I hope you're right."

"So do I," she said, too softly to be heard. She would never tell Isaiah that it was evident Toby knew exactly what to do with babies, children, women. He would do whatever he wanted with them. A flash of the lifeless body she had drug out of that very room flashed before her eyes. How was she going to keep it together?

They worked in silence the rest of the hour. Scrubbing the walls and floors, Loralye went over the room several times, making sure everything was as clean as it could be. She went over to the bucket of water and began to rinse out the washcloths in the murky pool.

Over and over, she let her rag fall to the bottom of the bucket. She would retrieve it, balancing the weight of the baby as she bent down and wrung the water out of the cloth. Over and over, she repeated the process methodically.

It wasn't until Isaiah came to her and placed his hand over hers that she stopped. "It's going to be okay; I know it will."

She snapped at him, "How do you know Isaiah? How can you say that when your life has been completely ruined down here?"

She regretted her words when she saw the tears filling his eyes. He did his best to look at her with a brave face. "My life has never been so good Miss Loralye, never."

She grabbed him in a motherly embrace, holding onto both him and the nestling baby sleeping soundly between them. She was also sorry that she had shown him her fear but didn't know how to stop the terrifying possibilities running through her mind.

"I'm so sorry Isaiah, I'm afraid they might take the baby, and I don't know what I will do if that happens."

"We can do something right now Loralye, something that is going to help."

"What can we do? We are locked down here, alone without a way out."

"We aren't alone at all. Miss Loralye, we have to pray."

"I can't pray to a God who has left me down here for so long anymore. How can he leave us here Isaiah? How can he let my baby grow up in this dark hole of hate?"

She kicked the bucket over, spilling the grimy water all over their clean floor. Embarrassed by her childish actions, she bent down to pick up the washrags that had floated around the room, the water carrying them as if they were limbs floating down a mighty river. How could she say those things to a young boy who was new in his faith? She was ashamed.

Before she could apologize, she looked over to see Isaiah on his knees. She would never forget the words that the little warrior prayed that day. "Lord, we don't see a way out of here, but You know the way. Just like with Moses, make a way for us, please. Keep baby Brew safe God, amen."

He got up, ran over to Loralye, and hugged her. Kissing Brew on his head, causing him to stir, he encouraged Loralye to talk with Toby. He told her that whatever happened, Jesus had already defeated death for them, just like she had said, and that was enough.

She knew he was right. Knew that Jesus dying for their sins was indeed enough. But when faced with the possibility of losing her only child, it felt like it wasn't. After cleaning up the mess she had made, Loralye walked Isaiah back to their room. Unwilling to take Abe into Toby's domain, Loralye decided to leave her son with Isaiah. She fed the baby and then entrusted him into Isaiah's arms.

Chapter Twenty-Four

"Come in Loralye," Toby said from behind his desk.

Loralye gingerly opened the door and sat in the chair across from the man she hated more and more each day. She readjusted herself, uncomfortable at the way the man was staring at her.

Toby sat back and placed his feet up on the desk. With his arms behind his head, he smirked at Loralye in a way that showed possession, and desire.

"Loralye, I must admit that I am surprised at your ability down here in the Hollow. I have had several members of the team ask me what I have changed to keep disease at bay down here in the past several weeks. We have had less sickness and less losses."

Unsure what to say, Loralye sat quietly and waited for him to continue. Placing his feet back on the ground, Toby sat towards her, his eyes locking with hers.

"What are your plans with the baby? Where is he?" he asked, glancing down at her chest. She wrapped her arms around herself uncomfortably.

"My plans are to do my job as well as I can down here Mr. Toby. I can take care of Brew while I do my job, I assure you."

She sat up a little straighter, faking a confidence she did not feel. "I left the baby with Isaiah. I didn't figure you wanted to meet with him as well."

He studied her for several moments, the attention causing Loralye to squirm in her chair. Toby broke his stare first, standing up, he walked over to his bar and poured himself a drink.

"I don't know why Loralye, but I find myself drawn to you. Your ability to have that baby down here and still get your work done today has proved me wrong in several ways. Porker has spoken very highly of you as well, and while I do not put too much stock in what he has to say, I do listen to his mumblings."

Loralye held her breath, as hope began to build up inside of her. She prayed that God was indeed hearing her.

Toby continued. "I believe that your idea of disinfecting the rooms is one that I want to expand upon. I have been throwing around the idea of having you oversee a team of three or four who could clean, not only the empty rooms but some of the others that are occupied."

"This isn't going to be an easy thing for you to handle Loralye. Not that I care how you feel. I just want you to be prepared for some of the things you are going to see. If you think what you have endured thus far has been tough, you're not going to make it."

He took a slow drink from his glass, watching her for signs of defeat. Loralye took a deep breath, as the anger she felt when she had dragged that poor little girl out of the room that very day, started bubbling within her. She wondered how things could be much worse. Would she be able to endure? Could she subject Isaiah and her newborn son to such evil?

Deciding that this may be her only opportunity, she needed to find out if she had any possibility of negotiating. "Mr. Toby, would this opportunity give me the ability to keep my child with me?"

He sat back down across from her, the power to separate the small family in his hands. "I believe that there may be ways for you to get what you want, if, I in turn can get what I want."

He got up and stood behind her. He started rubbing the back of her neck with his clammy hands, and chills ran down her spine as his mouth made contact with her neck. She screamed when he bit her shoulder, and her warm blood slid down her chest and soaked the uniform that had shrunk too tightly across her torso since she had begun to feed her baby.

Before she could push Toby away from her, Porker came barreling into the office. He grabbed Toby and threw him into the wall next to his bar. Toby looked at him with a smirk, as Loralye's blood dripped down his chin.

"Everything is all right Porker. We were just coming to an arrangement."

Porker looked from Loralye to Toby. The fear in her eyes created a rage inside of him that he had never felt before.

"Get out, now," Toby said as he wiped the warm liquid off his face.

Porker looked over at Loralye, a look of compassion passing across his face. He slowly left the room, closing the door behind him.

"I will deal with that later. Now, back to what I was saying. There is a way that you can keep your new baby with you, or if you would rather, I will add him to our program here, and you will still do what I want you to do. The choice is yours."

Loralye stared blankly at the far wall, unwilling to give him the respect of acknowledgment. Toby walked over to the door, locked it, and chuckled. Turning back towards her he said, "Good girl."

Chapter Twenty-Five

L oralye hobbled back to her room hours later. Her legs barely made it across the threshold. Her milk began to release as she heard Brew screaming through the door. She opened it slowly, and the site before her brought strength to her weakening body.

Isaiah walked around bouncing the baby up and down, singing one of the songs he had heard Loralye sing to the babe. She stood hunched over for a moment, the door jamb holding the brunt of her weight. She looked at her two boys and reminded herself of why she needed to fight for her life as long as she could.

When Isaiah's eyes met hers, he calmly took the baby to the bed, setting him down as carefully as you would a priceless possession. He then raced to Loralye. Holding her up with his small body, he pulled her close and walked her towards the screaming child. Without a word, he helped her into bed. Lifting her legs onto it, he then ran to the other side to move the baby close to her.

Loralye shushed the sweet little baby that screamed with all his might, as she nursed him back into the calm little one that she so loved. Her body ached as she lay on her side and satiated Brew's thirst. The torture from the hours before rolled back and forth in her mind. The love she had shared with her husband was nothing like what she had just experienced.

Her eyes closed as she lay there, warm tears sliding down her face unchecked. Isaiah continued to hum the same song he had been singing to the babe when she had first entered the room. The melody comforted Loralye, as if she were the one he was singing to, and she wondered if the song was intended for her.

She appreciated that Isaiah didn't ask about Toby, didn't ask why she came back bloodied and bruised. She felt the shame of the man crawling on her aching skin, and she figured Isaiah had guessed what had taken place. He didn't need her to voice it.

Brew fell asleep, his tummy full. Loralye lay there motionless, trying with all her might not to cry out in pain and disgust. How could she bear this relationship? She couldn't see a way out, couldn't see an end to the torture that only got worse as each day passed.

After a week of holding her baby, of loving the new life she had been entrusted with, she felt as though it had all been taken away. The automatic lights turned off, and the room was as dark as the darkest of nights. The three of them lay in the stillness, as Isaiah still hummed the lullaby that Loralye had learned from her mother. She fell into a fitful sleep, awakening the next morning to continue the nightmare that rivaled any dream she could have ever dreamt.

The next day, Loralye was surprised when they didn't get any assignments. Porker came in and told them that they had been given the day off. He left, embarrassed that he hadn't been able to save Loralye from his boss's desires.

Isaiah helped her to the chair, her muscles sore. He cleaned her wounds with a washcloth, bringing the baby to her for his feedings. Unsure how she would have made it without him, she was once again reminded of the good that was still present in this world.

The following morning, they went back to work. Loralye moved slower than usual, her body still recovering from birth, and from the evil man that she refused to acknowledge by name. Isaiah scrubbed the floors, forcing Loralye to sit for most of the day. She held tightly to her baby, thankful for the safe embrace that he gave, wrapped up snuggly against her.

When they were finished with the rooms they had been assigned, they went to put away their cleaning supplies in the locked closet. She smiled when she saw the two cookies left for them on a paper towel, obviously from Porker.

They enjoyed their sweet treat as they headed back to their room. Isaiah was licking the sugar off his fingers when Porker yelled for them to stop from behind.

"Wait a minute you two, we have one more job to do today."

Loralye's shoulders sagged at the thought of cleaning another room. Her body was broken, and she felt as if her legs could give out at any moment. How would she have the strength? She could not impose on Isaiah to do yet another room with the very little help she could offer.

Porker ran to catch up, sliding between them to continue the conversation.

"If you could follow me, I'll take you to the next assignment." He continued to babble on, not sensing the mood of the room.

They continued towards the room they called home. Loralye was surprised that there would be one to clean down this way because she and Isaiah had cleaned them weeks before the baby had come. She hadn't heard any screams from the hall either. How had she missed it?

"Should we stop and get our supplies Porker? We had thought our work was done for the day and we put everything away," Loralye asked.

Isaiah piped in, his voice chipper than her own. "Thanks for the cookies, Porker! Those were almost as good as the ones from Christmas."

"You're welcome, little man. I rescued those two before they were taken by the scoundrels in tunnel D. I wish I could have grabbed more, but there was only four when I got there. Since there's one of me and two of you, I decided I should probably eat two of them, so you didn't have to decide who got the last cookie."

Loralye had to smile at his logic, thankful he was walking with them and couldn't see the smirk she had been unable to hide.

Remembering that she too should thank him, she told him thank you as well. "Those were delicious and so appreciated after a hard day's work. Thank you for thinking of us Porker."

Not saying a word, his shoulders rose a little higher as the praise lifted his spirits as lofty as the ceilings would allow.

They stopped by the door next to their own. Porker took out his set of keys and unlocked it. He opened it and stepped aside, allowing Loralye and Isaiah to enter first. Her hand went up to her mouth, the shock of what sat before her causing her broken heart to shatter into another thousand pieces.

"Meet your new crew!" Porker said proudly from behind them as if he had just introduced them to a group of strong young men ready to scrub blood and dried feces off the floor, and not the young children that stared back at them, afraid and silent.

Isaiah inched towards the eight eyes that looked back at them. He knelt first beside the smallest of the group. "What's your name? I'm Isaiah," he said tenderly.

The oldest, a girl, looked at Loralye, noticing the baby that she held around her with the sheet that they had configured into a baby carrier. She walked over to her and rubbed the baby on his back softly. Her sweet young voice squeaked out just above a whisper, "I've never seen one like this."

Loralye prayed that the Lord would give her strength. Her heart couldn't handle the thought of anything happening to this sweet girl, who had instantly made her way into her heart with just a few words.

Chapter Twenty-Six

The little girl rubbed Brew's back so gently that Loralye was unsure if her little hands had made contact. She smiled and went back to the other children and sat down beside them. Loralye looked at the small work crew that anxiously watched her. Two of the four children were too timid to look up, and Loralye could sense their fear and uncertainty.

Sadness took hold of Loralye as she looked at the children sitting on the cold concrete floor. She started putting a barricade up around her heart, the fear of loss growing with every step she took; One step, brick. Two steps, two bricks. She was going to have to build a wall that would reach a mile high so they would not be able to break through.

The little girl that had been so enthralled with Brew looked up at her with her large brown eyes. Her brown hair had been cut short, and the little she did have was matted together and unwashed. As soon as the girl looked down at Brew, Loralye felt one of the bricks she had just put in place fall away.

"Lord help me," she whispered, terrified at the thought that these children were stuck down there in the Hollow with her.

Isaiah knelt by a boy that couldn't have been more than five years old. He tussled his dirty blonde hair and the boy jerked away from him, getting out of arms reach.

"I'm sorry friend, I'm not going to hurt you. My name is Isaiah, what's yours?"

The boy looked up from the floor for a second before moving his eyes back to the ground. He didn't say anything. The brown-eyed girl put her arm around him before saying, "This is James. He and I are buds, aren't we?"

James looked at her, his eyes smiling up in a comfortable, familiar way. He didn't say anything but placed his hand in hers, his head leaning against her shoulder. She patted him in a motherly way with her free hand before continuing with introductions.

"My name is Liz. That's Seth, and that girl over there, she is new. I don't know her name yet." She gently pushed away from James and leaned towards the little girl who sat cross-legged in front of her.

"What's your name anyways? I'm Liz."

The girl leaned close and whispered something no one could quite hear. "Can you whisper a little louder? I can't hear you very well." She edged nearer and whispered again, a little louder into Liz's ear. Loralye grew eager to hear the little one's name, her black hair falling in whisps around either side of her face.

"Ah, what a great name! Everyone, this is Fay. Fay, this is everyone! Well, I don't exactly know everyone. What's your name anyway lady?" she asked, looking at Loralye.

"And what is that little one's name? I have never seen anything so small." Liz's eyes got glossy as she took in Abe's little face poking out the side of his carrier.

Loralye tried to angle him so he could be seen well. She got on her knees in front of the group to introduce herself and her son at eye level.

"My name is Loralye, and this little guy, this is Abe. We call him Brew though. He is my son, and a little less than two weeks old."

Loralye hadn't thought about the fact that she hadn't been able to show off her baby the way that she would have liked to. Her neighbors would have come over and met the new addition, bringing meals and gifts to welcome the new bundle into the community.

The older ladies at church would have loved his chubby feet and long fingers. She imagined Abe, holding him at the front of the church, and dedicating him to the Lord. Oh, what she wouldn't give to go back in time and change the course of her future, and that of her sons.

Trying to leave the could haves, and the should haves behind, she continued with her introductions. Smiling with pride, she took Isaiah by the hand and said, "And this young man here, this is Isaiah. He is a wonderful friend to me down here, and I know that he will be a wonderful friend to you all as well."

Loralye heard Porker clear his throat from behind, and she smiled. She stood up and walked over to him. "And this, this here is Porker. He's a new friend and has been a God send for sure."

She bent towards the children, still standing next to Porker, and in a loud whisper said, "He brings us cookies sometimes," just loud enough for the room of attentive ears to hear. At the mention of cookies, every eye looked up.

Porker laughed and slapped his knee. "That's right! I do that for sure. I'll bring ya's all some tonight if I can get my hands on em'. Would you like that?"

They all nodded excitedly. Little James licking his lips at the thought of having the sugary treat. Porker took that as a yes and then told the group he would bring them to Loralye and Isaiah's room as soon as he had time.

"Speaking of time, I got things to do. You follow me and I'll be back in a few hours."

Loralye and Isaiah got up and walked toward the door. The four children sat there, unmoving, and unsure of what to do. Isaiah went back to the group and urged them to follow.

"Come on guys, it will be ok, I promise. Miss Loralye is real nice. She reads stories from the Bible. Some aren't in there, cause the Bible she has doesn't have all the books. Some she tells from what she remembers. Maybe we could get her to tell us a real good one for your first night. Miss Loralye, could you tell us the story of David and Goliath tonight? Please?"

"Of course, I can. Come along now children. I'm not like the other grownups down here. I would love to tell you a story, if, that is, you like stories."

Liz was the first one to stand up, taking charge of the ones that were still sitting. "Come on guys. I like her, and I like that baby. She can't be takin' us anywhere worse than where we was. Come on James, Fay, and Seth. Member that guy might bring us cookies too." At the reminder of cookies, the rest of them got to their feet.

They followed behind Porker to the door next to the room they had just left. Porker locked them inside, promising that he would be back at dinner time with the promised cookies and a meal. The group found a corner of the room and sat down, all except Liz.

Loralye took a seat in the only chair, her body aching from the day's work. She unwrapped the baby, who had just started to squirm and began to nurse him. Liz, who had been inching herself closer to the duo every few moments asked, "What are you doing with your baby under there?"

She pointed to the sheet that was covering Brew, his little feet poking out of the side of the sheet. Loralye smiled, thankful for the opportunity to share more of her priceless treasure.

"Right now, I'm feeding him his dinner."

Liz accepted her answer by shaking her head as if she understood what Loralye was talking about. Loralye chuckled, knowing full well that she had no idea what Brew could possibly be eating underneath a thin sheet cover.

Taking the opportunity to share, Loralye waved at Liz to get closer. She let her peek in at the nestling babe. "See, he's drinking his milk right now."

Liz took a step back, having never seen anything as amazing as that. A look of wonder crossed her face. "I never saw nothin' like that," she said amazed.

"It's pretty special, isn't it? God made us to be able to take care of our children all on our own. Bottles are wonderful, and a blessing to those who cannot nurse their own babies, but the ability to supply every need Brew has, is a blessing to my mama's heart."

"Can I ask you a question Miss Loralye?"

"Of course, you can."

"Who is God? And what's a mama's heart?"

Loralye smiled sadly. She did everything she could to keep the tears at bay. It would never cease to amaze her at the small things that these poor souls didn't know, the things they had never heard of. Deciding to take on the easier of the two questions first, Loralye told her what a mama's heart was.

"A mama's heart is something that happens when you have a baby. It is like you get a whole new one. Your old one gets replaced with a special heart that is made just for your baby. It's very special." She moved the sheet back and peeked at Brew, her heart swelling at the site of the perfect bundle she held.

"Now, on to your other question. God is that special One who gives away mama's hearts. He made you, and me, and James, Fay, and Seth. He designed each of us exactly right, taking His time and counting all the hairs on our heads. He loves us very much and is

162

everywhere all at once. You cannot see Him, but He is here just the same."

Liz tried to take in what Loralye was saying, but she was confused. The thought of someone named God there with them, watching them but unable to be seen Himself, was more than she could comprehend.

"Are you sure this God see's everything?"

"I am."

"And He's the one who changes these mama's hearts and stuff?"

"That's right."

Liz sat on the edge of the bed. Her mind deep in thought. Loralye finished nursing the baby and burped him on her shoulder. His eyes closed and he fell asleep, his little muscles giving in to complete relaxation. Knowing that she had just given out a lot of information for anyone to take in, let alone a child, Loralye asked what Liz was thinking.

"I was just thinking that this God forgot about changing my mamas' heart."

Loralye winced at her blunder. How could she have been so insensitive to the poor child? 'How do I fix this Lord?' she silently prayed. Deciding that honesty was always the best, even when it hurt, she knew she had to tell Liz the truth.

"Sometimes, God offers these special hearts to people, and they don't want them. They keep their old ones, and the old ones weren't designed to be mama's. I am so sorry that your mama didn't take her new heart Liz. I am so sorry."

Liz stared blankly at the wall across the room. Loralye looked over to the three others who were being occupied by Isaiah's yoyo tricks. She was grateful he had thought to keep them entertained.

Knowing this could be her only opportunity, not knowing what the next day would bring especially down in the Hollow, Loralye continued to talk about the gift God offers freely to all.

"Liz, did you know that just because your mama didn't want her new heart, that does not mean that it was anything you did. God designed you to be perfect the way you are, but He does not make anyone take their new hearts If they don't want them. They must decide to take it themselves."

"Why would He give them a choice?" she said, tears streaming down her cheeks.

"Why would He not make mamas take their new hearts? Why didn't He make my mama want to keep me?"

Loralye got up from her chair slowly, her body aching with every move of her muscles. She sat next to Liz and carefully placed Brew in her arms. Liz continued to cry but the tears did slow. She was mesmerized by the small form in her arms.

"God gives us all a choice because He loves us. I'm sure you have had to do things that you did not want to do down here. So, have I. We haven't had a choice in those matters. Wouldn't it be nice if we did?"

Liz nodded. The thoughts of all the things she would not have chosen to have gone through, racing through her mind.

"God has blessed us with the choice of taking on a new heart. That is one of the greatest gifts He has ever supplied. The freedom to choose Him or walk away from Him.

"Sadly, many choose to walk away, to not take that new heart he made especially for us. When people choose that way, that's when this happens." She swept her arm across the room, encompassing the Hollow, and the hate and hardness that imprisoned them.

Not looking up from Brew whose little fist now held tightly to one of Liz's fingers, she said just loud enough to hear, "I'm glad that I get to choose. It might be the only thing I ever get to pick."

Loralye prayed that she would indeed choose a soft, warm heart filled to the brim with God's love. She also prayed that she would be able to show that heart even when she didn't understand the whys of what she was going through.

Chapter Twenty-Seven

Porker came as he promised, holding in his hand a box filled with food and cookies for everyone. Loralye wondered why sometimes he could bring real meals, and other times he only had a jar of peanut butter. She was glad that tonight was a night he had a real meal.

The four new children ate as if they were starving. The soft bread was gone in seconds as the children soaked it in their meat and potato soup. The cookies were gobbled up as if they had never tasted sugar before, and Loralye wondered if maybe they hadn't.

She tucked her cookie away for them for later, knowing they would enjoy it more than she would. They sat in a circle on the floor, as Porker kept them entertained with stories of how he had once saved a cat from one of the tunnels.

He had named him Sprinkles, and he still slept in Porker's room to this day. He said he would bring him by sometime.

After he left for the evening, Loralye tried to learn more about each child. Liz was without a doubt the one in charge. She had many qualities that reminded Loralye of Isaiah and knew that she was going to be a tremendous help.

Isaiah gravitated to the younger children, Fay, James, and Seth. James was quiet but loved Isaiah's red yo-yo. Loralye was thankful for the toy and the bond that it was forming between them. James laughed as Isaiah cat walked the yoyo across the floor and the sound filled the room with a lightness that brought smiles to everyone.

Loralye sat with Liz and the other children and tried to ask them some questions about their past. "So, how long have you been down here in the Hollow?"

Liz looked up from the baby that Loralye had resting on her shoulder with such an intense stare, that Loralye wondered if Liz could see the same pain reflected in her eyes that Loralye saw in hers.

Liz sat there, staring for several moments, weighing the cost of sharing her story. After what felt like an eternity, she decided that it was worth the risk to be vulnerable one more time.

"When I was younger, I wasn't down here in this dark, cold hole. I can't remember a bunch, but I remember the sun and the rain. I remember ice cream and jump ropes."

Her eyes rested once on Abe, relishing the innocence he still had. She wondered how long he would keep it down here.

"I can't remember all of what happened, but here is what I do remember. My mama didn't want me, didn't care about me. She would be gone all night sometimes, and I would hide under her bed afraid and alone. I never met my dad, at least if I did, I don't remember it.

"I do remember the last time I saw her. I heard the car pull up to the house and I was so excited to see her, I climbed out from under her bed and ran to the door. I remember seeing the lights from the car travel along the wall. She came in with a man I had never seen before. She didn't say a word to me, even though I screamed at her and tried to hug her. She pushed me off her leg and went into her room. That man forced me into his car and brought me down here, and I never saw my mom again."

Loralye's heart ached for the girl. She looked at her baby and wondered how any mother could treat their child like that. She couldn't imagine losing Brew, couldn't imagine choosing to give him up.

"I'm so sorry you had to go through that Liz, that's not the way things are supposed to be."

Liz shook it off, as if her mother had simply forgotten to wish her a happy birthday, and not thrown her to the wolves.

"It's ok, I'm over it. I can't really remember much of her anyway. She never spent time with me and is probably glad I'm gone."

"How old are you?"

"I don't rightly know. I was smaller than James when I got here, and I'm not sure how long ago that was."

"Where were you before Porker brought you here today?"

Liz looked away. Her shoulders fell, and her confidence waned. Loralye thought she saw her shoulders shake in fear but couldn't be sure. Liz immediately pulled herself back together, not allowing the terror to control her.

"I have been in the pickin' rooms."

"What are those?"

"Are you sure you want to know?"

Loralye nodded her head.

"The room I was in was about the size of this one. There was ten of us in there. James and Seth were two of them. I was the tallest, so probably the oldest. We had two beds to share, one sink, and a hole for a toilet just like you have here.

"I hated being in there. When they asked for volunteers to leave, I was the first one to raise my hand. I feel bad for leaving the others, but I couldn't be sure where I was going. I didn't know if it was going to be better or worse than where we were. I didn't care. I thought anything would be better than that place."

"What happened in the picking room, Liz," Loralye asked gently.

She took a deep breath, her gaze resting on the wall across from where she sat. She placed her hands under her legs, her feet dangling off the bed. Her body began to rock back and forth, her face began to redden.

"We never knew how long we would go before one of the men would come in. We would hear the keys rattle in the lock. The younger kids would all try to hide behind me. Sometimes food would be brought in, and the other times..."

Liz paused, unable to get the words out. After a moment to compose herself, she said, "Those was the bad times."

Loralye stayed silent, giving her the time she needed, before she shared the rest of her story.

"I remember the first time I was picked. That time, I was considered special, I guess, because I had never been picked before. That time, I was put in a fancy room with a fancy bed. They tied me down. I didn't know why. I screamed for my mom, but of course, she never came. It was silly of me to yell I suppose. She wouldn't have come even if she had heard me," she said matter-of-factly.

"That time, the man that came was in a fancy suit. He beat me and then did what you're thinking he did. I couldn't walk for lots of days. They had an older kid come in, like my age now, and take care of me. After that, I would get picked from the picking room every few days. Since I have gotten older, I get picked less and less. Now I help take care of the little ones more. I help them when they can't take care of themselves when they're hurt."

"I'm so sorry that you have had to go through so much in your short years Liz, truly I am."

Liz wiped away the tears that were sliding unchecked down her cheeks. Her chapped skin was flaking like scales hiding the soft skin underneath.

"Why are you sorry? You didn't abandon me, didn't lock me down here. Life ain't easy and it never will be for any of us."

Loralye wanted to tell her that wasn't true, that they still might have a life full of love and happiness. But if she were honest with herself, she couldn't say that, couldn't place that spark of hope in her heart or Liz's. Just as Jonah was in the belly of a whale, there was no way they would escape this dark hell unless God Himself caused the whale of the Hollow to spit them back up on dry ground.

They sat there and watched the other children play, the silence between them companionable. They understood what each other was going through. They understood that they were both stuck. The saying misery loves company crossed Loralye's mind, but that wasn't quite right. She wasn't glad that Liz or any of the others were suffering with her. What she was thankful for was that they could all lean on one another during their imprisonment.

Liz looked over at Fay who was laughing at Isaiah, now on all fours pretending to be Porker's cat. She smiled. "When I raised my hand to volunteer, James and Seth raised their hands as soon as they saw me raise mine. They are my buds."

"I can see how much they love you. What about Fay? You said she was new?"

"Yeah, she's new all right. She had just come from one of the fancy rooms, so she couldn't have been here more than a few nights. We'll have to try to get her to tell her story. I don't know it."

A lot of things were beginning to make sense to Loralye. Why Liz was the leader, why Fay was quiet, and why the boys followed Liz around like a mother hen. Liz was a commander, who, even down in this hole, was able to help the younger children. In many ways, she had become a mother to them.

Loralye watched Liz as she watched the three young children play with Isaiah. Liz's face turned from gloom to joy, the smile inside her shining brightly. "You love them, don't you Liz?"

Liz's smile faded, her eyes coming back to Loralye's. "Love is hard to understand. Love hurts. You wouldn't believe how many kids I have seen not come back when they get picked. It's hard every time."

"Yet you still help the new ones, don't you? Even though you know it Is going to hurt if they leave and you don't see them again?" Liz nodded.

"You know that reminds me of someone I know very well. Children, come on over here," Loralye said to the four across the room. They all came quickly and sat in front of her.

"Are you going to tell us about David and Goliath?"

"I will in a minute. First, I want to tell you all about a man named Jesus."

Chapter Twenty-Eight

After Loralye had shared some stories about Jesus, she was surprised when Seth was the first one to say anything. "This Jesus sounds pwety neat. I wish I could walk on water too."

She smiled, agreeing whole heartedly that Jesus was indeed spectacular. "One day Seth, maybe we will be able to do just that."

"How can I do that when the only waters we gots here is in that sink." He pointed to the dripping sink in the corner of the room.

Loralye smiled, loving the way his mind worked, and the curiosity that he showed. She would never tire of how little minds worked. "That is a great question, Seth. One day, we won't be here anymore. We will be in Heaven with Jesus. Because He never changes, I believe that He still walks on water, and I hope that He asks me to walk with Him when I see Him face to face."

Liz piped in, "How will He get us out of here and to this heaven where we will be able to 'walk on water?' I have been down here for a long time, and I have searched and searched for a way out. How is He going to get us out? He has never even been here."

Loralye took a deep breath. The questions of how were sometimes the most challenging to answer.

"I know that it's hard to understand, but Jesus has been here. He is here even now."

Surprised, the children started looking around, trying to find the man who was going to help them escape. Little James went and looked under the bed, and Isaiah covered his mouth to try and hide his laughter.

Isaiah stood up and shook his head as if they should know what Loralye was talking about. In his sure tone, he tried to explain. "Guys, Jesus is right here, in my heart and in Loralye's. He lives in here" he said, as he patted his chest over his heart to emphasize what he was saying.

"When you ask Jesus to come, He will. Then He will never leave you. You never are alone. He will speak to you too and guide you. You all should ask Him to come now so He can be in your hearts too!" Isaiah was getting increasingly animated, his excitement contagious.

Fay, James, and Seth all grabbed ahold of Isaiah's words. They were all standing now, eager to invite Jesus into their hearts. Liz, however, was hesitant. Being the oldest and being through the most, Loralye wasn't surprised that she wasn't blindly ready to believe in an invisible Man that would come into her heart and one day take her out of this evil place.

"Isaiah, why don't you take these three over there and help them invite Jesus into their hearts," Loralye said, excited for Isaiah to be able to be a part of their redemption story. She turned her attention back to Liz.

"Liz, can I answer any questions for you? You look like you just got done taking your school exams." She placed a hand on her shoulder and smiled.

Liz crossed her arms as if protecting herself from the possible hope that was being offered. Wiggling out of Loralye's embrace, she said what was on her mind, not ashamed of the way she was thinking.

"I just don't understand why someone who is supposed to care for us so much, would leave us down here like this."

Loralye knew exactly that very feeling. She asked herself the same question daily and hoped that she could help Liz see the love that Christ had for her.

"I know that what you have gone through is hard, and we may never know, while we are on this earth, why we have been put in such a hellish place. I often wonder what I did to deserve being down here myself." Absentmindedly, she reached up and gingerly touched her neck, still able to feel the indentations of Toby's teeth.

"What I do know, is that Jesus was perfect in every way, and He by no means deserved being placed on that cross for me. But He still chose to take our sins on Himself so we could be washed white as snow, even though we don't deserve it. If a perfect person had to suffer and die to save us from our sin, then bein' an imperfect person myself, having to go through hard things, is just part of my story."

"Why do you believe in Someone who would let you live your life like this?" Liz asked.

"Well, to be honest, I just do. He has shown Himself to me in so many ways, there is no way my mind could not believe. If I decided not to follow Him, I would be doing myself a disservice as well as Him. If I am going to be going through my life like this, why wouldn't I want the King of Kings to go with me?"

"I just don't think that He could be real. You're telling me that the One who created the earth, wants to live in my heart and protect me, wants to be with me wherever I go? I am just not buying it." She looked over at Isaiah who was praying over each of the children, a loving smile on his face.

"That's ok Liz, you don't have to decide right now. Just know that as soon as you are ready to invite Him in, He will come."

"Sure, yeah that's great," Liz said, in a monotone and disinterested voice.

"If you ever have any questions about it, I'm here."

"Okay, thanks."

Loralye would have to pray that God became real to Liz. Sadly, where they were, there was no way to know how many days they had left, before it would be too late.

New York, New York Present Day

Kay and Carter sat down late into the night. The notebook from Andrea laying open in between them. Carter had Google maps opened to one of the locations in New York on his laptop, hoping to see an entry point to one of the tunneling systems.

"I just don't see where these entries could be. This looks like it's just a small neighborhood. Families live here."

Kay looked at the area where Carter was pointing. The screen zoomed in on different areas of the city that he had plugged in.

"Remember the house I was scoping out?" She asked.

"You mean the one that almost got you killed? Yes, I remember," Carter said.

The pain remembering how near he came to losing her snapped him to attention. He couldn't go through that again.

Months before, Kay had followed a lead to a small house in a neighboring street. A man, part of the underground trafficking organization she had been trying to expose, had deliberately caused a terrible car accident. She had survived but had lost the ability of ever having children of her own. Her shoulders shuddered involuntarily at the memory.

"Well, that was just a house that had a basement. No one would ever have thought that it was the entrance to an underground child trafficking ring. We need to start looking at more unconventional entry points."

Carter nodded his head, thinking that Kay was probably right.

"It's not as it seems. Maybe we should send some teams to scout a few areas and see if they come up with anything."

"Yes! I love that idea. Let's put Al in charge of getting a few teams up and running and scope out the areas that are close to home first. Then we can move on to further out locations. We need to keep this as quiet as possible. I do not want to take any chances of someone finding out about it.

"Let's call him now. I don't want to wait," Kay said. Getting up from her spot on the floor, she was excited at the thought of bringing this darkness into the light.

"Babe, its two a.m. We could wait until morning to ask him. You know Al. If we call and wake him up this late, he will panic, thinking you are in danger. Then, once he knows you are safe, he will jump on this full force. Maybe we need to let everyone have a full night of rest before conquering this evil."

She sighed, knowing he was right. "I'm just so ready to get down there and bring justice to those children. Every day we wait, more kids are getting taken, getting hurt. It makes me sick thinking that if we wait, another child will suffer."

"If we jump the gun, they could close down a tunneling system, and we will not get them all. It's going to benefit us to wait until we are ready to go in from as many angles as we can."

"I know you're right. It's just so hard to wait."

"I know it is. But Gods timing is perfect, every single time."

The baby monitor blinked as Hope began to cry. The light of the monitor grabbed Kay's attention first.

"Saved by the bell I suppose. I'll get Hope. Will you make her a bottle?"

"Yes, I will. Let's get her back to sleep and try to get a few hours of sleep ourselves. I have a feeling that we are about to spend many hours wide awake."

Knowing he was right, Kay resolved to get as much rest as she could. Whatever was going to happen in the next few weeks, was going to happen in God's timing, not her own.

"Lord, protect as many of them as you can until we can get there," she said, as she pulled Hope out of the crib and into her loving arms.

Chapter Twenty-Nine

Carter woke up and reached over to wake up Kay, but she wasn't there. He looked at the clock on his bedside table: 6:07 a.m. He threw his legs over the side of the bed to find out why his wife was not still asleep. He was not surprised to find her in the office on the phone.

The baby was asleep in her bouncer, and Kay rocked it in a slow rhythm with her foot. She was holding her phone between her ear and shoulder as she simultaneously typed something on the computer. She looked away from the screen and smiled at him as he took the seat across from her. Carter wondered how long she had been able to wait before calling Al and hoped that he had at least gotten a few hours of sleep.

"Al, I am telling you we need more than ten teams. No, I do not know where you're going to find that many people, that's your job. Can't you get in touch with some of your old army friends? I bet they all have been waiting for something exciting to be a part of again. Yes, I want you to call them."

Carter laughed, as he listened to the friendly banter between the two of them. He couldn't ask for a better person to protect his wife. Al would find the teams she wanted, and if he knew him at all, they would be ready to go tonight.

After she got off the phone, Kay took her foot off the bouncer and walked over to her smiling husband. She climbed onto his lap in her shorts and long cozy socks.

"What happened to a good night's sleep love?" he asked, inhaling the scent of her hair as she leaned into him.

"Babe, hear me out. I slept for like two hours before a dream woke me up. I had to get started planning right away, this just can't wait."

"What was your dream?"

"I am so glad you asked. You and I were watching teams going to different entry points from some sort of monitor. There were dozens of them on the screen."

"So that explains the call to Al," he said.

"Exactly. I don't know how we are going to do it, but we need to go in as many entrances as we can at the same time."

"What else was in the dream?"

"You're going to think I'm crazy. There was a calendar with a date circled."

He took a deep breath. "When Kay?"

"Seven days from now." She pulled away from his chest, looking deeply into his eyes. Carter brushed away a loose strand of hair away from her face, tucking it behind her ear.

"We can do it, Carter. I just know that we can do it."

He kissed her before pulling her back into himself. "I know we can Love."

She sat up again, surprised at his answer.

"Well, here I was thinking that I would have to talk you into this. I spent the better part of an hour going through what I would say when you told me no."

He laughed. "I'm not that easy to read, am I?"

"Sorry babe. One thing I love about you is that you are consistent. You don't like to make quick moves and never have."

"True."

"I have to ask. Why are you agreeing to this so soon? Not that I mind, you understand, I'm relieved that we are moving forward so quickly. I'm just surprised."

Carter laughed, but then became very serious.

"I just don't even know how to say this. My mind still can't believe it, but Kay, last night I had a dream too. The number seven kept flashing in my dream. Everywhere I looked; seven, seven, seven. If you ask me, seven days has been confirmed. We will be ready to go in seven days, and God is going to do whatever He has planned."

Kay kicked her feet in excitement.

"I am going to call Al back! Maybe he has some answers for me."

She leaped off Carter's lap, anxious to find out if Al was ready to go on the mission of a lifetime, along with dozens of teams.

"I don't think he is going to have everything ready quite yet Kay. Let's give him at least an hour."

"Ugh. Fine! I will give him one hour, but that's it."

She took out the notebook Andrea had given them and again went over the information inside. Ready or not, in seven days, they would be making the biggest move in trafficking history. Later that evening, Al came over with several aerial views of the various locations they were looking at throughout the state of New York.

"I have twenty-eight teams who will be ready to move in a week. We have an Infrared video being set up as we speak at these locations. Most of them are here in New York. I have one set up in Ohio, and two in California. There are over three hundred locations in that notebook you gave me. I wish we could cover them all."

"Me too. But this is a great start. If we can get this to hit the press and stick, law enforcement will have no choice but to help," Kay said, her thoughts running thousands of miles an hour.

"I think you're right," Al said. "If there is enough publicity on this, and if we can make the other locations public, the police, CIA, and special ops will have no choice but to help. If they don't, the public is going to figure out that they had a part in this."

"Exactly."

Carter came into the dining room where they had everything laid out on the table, a plate of cookies in his hand.

"I made some oatmeal raisin cookies Al. I thought I heard you say those were your favorite."

"Yes, they are, thank you."

Al took one from the top of the pile, and Kay declined. Bringing the cookie up to his mouth, Al took a big bite of his favorite dessert, but spit it out as soon as it entered his mouth.

"Carter, I can't eat this."

"It can't be that bad," Carter said before picking one of the cookies up and tasting it for himself.

He did not say anything, as he too spat out the bite of cookie he had eaten. He placed the plate in front of Al, before putting the rest of his cookie on the platter. He then picked the platter up and calmly took it back into the kitchen.

Kay and Al burst out laughing when they heard him say, "Martha makes it look so easy! I would not force a dog to try this. Sorry Al," he yelled over his shoulder.

"It's the thought that counts," Al yelled back. "If you get a bill in the mail for a chipped tooth, this is why."

"Fair enough," Carter shouted back from the kitchen. Kay heard the trash can open before the clunk of hard as rock cookies fell to the bottom of the receptacle.

Kay ordered pizza from their favorite spot before they got back to work.

"So, tell me, where did you find so many teams so quickly?"

"Well, you were right. My buddies were more than ready for their next assignment. Not only did everyone I called agree, but I also had a few of them whose sons are in the service, who offered to set up teams of their own. They don't know all the details, just that the Governor needs their help."

"That's perfect. Now, let's discuss which teams will be going where."

The team of three worked late into the night, eating pizza, and deciding the fate of each team that they would be sending down into the tunnels, hidden beneath the cities they had grown up in.

The next morning, Al came downstairs almost jogging down each step. Staying so late the night before, Kay had begged him to use their guest room instead of going across town at 3 a.m. He sat down at the dining room table where Carter and Kay waited for him with cups of coffee and scones.

"Want a scone?" Carter asked as he poured Al a cup of coffee from the carafe that sat in the center of the table.

"Did you make them?" Al asked as he took a sip from the piping hot black coffee.

Kay covered her mouth, trying to keep the laughter at bay.

"No, I did not. Kay's brother Saul heard that we have had a few late nights and brought coffee and scones early this morning. He took Hope to his house for the day as well, so we can get more work done before tomorrow."

"In that case, I would love a scone," Al said, as he took one of the perfectly soft blueberry scones off the ceramic serving tray. The lemon glaze coated his fingers, the taste of sweet and sour hitting all the right notes.

"That was the best scone I have ever had."

"You should try their muffins. Ah-mazing," Kay said with a singsong voice that expressed the joy she was feeling. Al and Carter could both see that she was lighter than she had been in months. The weight of the lost children had taken its toll on her. With the end in sight, her whole demeanor was beginning to change.

"Well, I just got off the phone with a buddy of mine who had an idea I wanted to bring to the table," Al said as he wiped his sticky fingers on one of the printed napkins.

"I'm listening," Kay said.

"What if we called the people to help us guard the entrances of each of these tunnels? A national militia of sorts."

"I mean, on the surface that sounds like a great idea," Kay said. "But who could we ask to do that? Who could we trust? Who do we know that are honest and on the right side of wanting the children to be set free?"

Al leaned onto the table and looked from Carter to Kay, making sure he had their full attention.

"We ask the ones that know what it means to lose one. I want to ask the dads of every missing child in America."

Chapter Thirty

Underground, February 1964

Loralye and her crew worked hard every day to keep up with Toby's demands. She wondered what they had done before she and her team cleaned the rooms, baffled that no one had done this before. The team had to split up to get everything done each day. She and the two young boys were in one group and Isaiah, Liz, and Fay in the other.

One day, while she was working in one of the larger rooms with the boys, Toby came into the room, gaining the attention of the trio. "Well, well, well. Looks like you are all working hard."

The boy's cowered behind Loralye. She did her best not to show the disgust that she held for this man. "Yes, we are Mr. Toby. What can we do for you," she asked, as she put a protective arm around Brew who was nestled close to her in his carrier. Her other arm reached behind her to offer comfort to the boys.

"Come to my office when you're through. Leave the baby." He walked out of the room, head held high.

"Are you okay Miss Loralye?" James asked, peering around from behind his hiding place.

"I'll be fine little one," she said, praying that was the truth.

"I only ask, cause your leg is shaking."

She looked down, noticing that he was right. Doing her best to still herself, she smiled at him and went back to work. Humming

184

an old hymn, she tried not to think about what Toby might be 'needing' from her.

When their work was finished, she took the boys back to their room and fed the baby. When Isaiah and Liz finished for the day, and were in the room with the others, she left them in charge. She placed Brew into Liz's arms and went to find out what Toby wanted.

Loralye stood at his door a long while before gaining the courage to knock. "Come in," he said from the other side.

She sat in her usual chair, biting on her bottom lip to keep it still. Unwilling to speak, she waited for Toby to finish whatever he was reading from the other side of the desk. When he finished his article, he sat the book down and looked up.

"Loralye, we are very pleased with the work you are doing. You have trained those kids and brought a lot of peace to my superiors. Disease is down, the smell down here is tolerable, and we are incredibly pleased indeed."

"Thank you, sir."

"We are wanting to move into other areas of the business with this change. There are other regions down here that are more sensitive than others. I do not know that your young ones will be able to endure some of them, and still continue to get their work done."

He stood up and walked over to his bar and poured himself a drink. "I want you to assign one of them to watch your baby."

Her back stiffened. She didn't want to be without Brew. "But sir," he walked over and slapped her before she could say another word.

"You will do as I say, or I will take him and the others away from you. Do you understand?"

She raised her hand to her burning cheek. Without looking up, she said, "Yes sir."

"That's more like it. As I was saying. I want you to assign one of them to watch the baby. You and the older boy are going to be moving to this other area to work. It's a far walk, and you will be gone most of the day. I have spoken with Porker, and he is working on getting formula down here for the baby for when you are away."

Loralye did her best not to cry. Her breasts began to ache as if they knew what it was going to be like not to nurse Brew all day long. He went on, "You will get one day off a week to rest. What day would you like?"

"Sunday," she said immediately, not needing any time to think about it.

"Very well. You and Isaiah will get Sundays off. The rest of them will continue to sanitize rooms as needed. If things start to slack off, and they don't get done, in a timely manner, I will send them all back to where they were before. Do you understand?"

She nodded.

"Very good. Porker will take you to the scare floor tomorrow morning. Make sure you prepare yourself. If you can't handle it, the baby will be taken, and you will become a part of that place."

She shuddered as worry filled her from the top of her head to the souls of her feet.

"I will be able to handle it, sir," she said, praying that she told the truth. Fear gripped her heart as she wondered exactly what the "scare room" was.

"I know you will. You're a survivor Loralye, we all see it. That's why you have made it here as long as you have. I believe you were made for these conditions."

"Thank you, sir," she said, wondering how anyone could be made for this place.

"I will go tell the children what is expected." She stood up and walked towards the closed door, hoping to leave the room as quickly as possible.

"Woah now, what's the big hurry," Toby said as he came from behind her. He rubbed her arm from shoulder to elbow, and her face began to burn again where he had hit her just moments before.

"We still have," he paused, turning her to face him forcefully. He threw her into the door, the weight of his body pressing into the heavy wood. He leaned into her, his breath against her ear as he whispered, "Other matters to discuss."

She closed her eyes and prayed that someone would save her. No one did. When Toby was finished, Loralye walked back to her room, sore and used. She was thankful that there were no visible marks to have to explain this time, and that her pain was hidden, to bear alone.

When she got back to her room, she took Brew out of Liz's arms and nursed him. After Porker had brought their dinner, a bottle, and formula, she told the children of the changes to come.

"That's not fair," Liz said, standing and pacing the room. They had all grown close over the past month. The comradery between them growing more and more each day.

"Life isn't fair little one, it never will be," Loralye said, brushing the coarse curls on top of her baby's head.

"What about that God of yours? Can't you ask Him to do something?"

"I thought you didn't believe in him?" James said, his voice raised and cracking with fear of the change.

"I don't!" Liz retorted. "But if I'm wrong, and you all are right, isn't this something you could ask Him for?"

"We can ask all we want. That doesn't mean that we'll get it though. His ways are higher than ours. We see things so magnified in the moment. God has seen the end from the beginning, and He knows why we are here, and how long we need to stay. Asking is something we can do, but that does not mean He will answer the way we want."

Loralye rocked the baby in the new rocking chair that Porker had so thoughtfully brought, as the truth of her words settled in her own heart.

"I just don't understand why this is happening," Liz said as she paced the floor, her hands raising up and down in frustration.

"We finally have a routine. I don't mind what I'm doing, and now everything's changing!" She fell onto the bed, as her hands covered her face.

Loralye stood and handed the baby to Isaiah. Sitting beside Liz, she pulled her into her embrace.

"I know, dear friend, that change is hard. Our lives have been flipped upside down. It doesn't make sense, it doesn't seem fair, and yet, I guarantee it is all for a purpose."

"What purpose could possibly be met by us being divided like this," Liz said, as she wiped her eyes with the back of her hand.

"I wish I could answer that. It's not for us to know the whys of life. What our purpose is, is to take whatever we are thrown into and show the love of Jesus. Remember when I told you about Joseph in the Bible and his beautiful coat? Remember what I said about his brothers?"

"Yeah, I remember. But those are just stories."

"They aren't just stories Liz. One day you will believe that. I am sure that Joseph wondered why things were changing when his brothers faked his death and sold him into slavery. If only he knew then what his purpose was. He was going to save the nation, including his brothers, from a famine that swept across the land."

Liz looked at the wall on the other side of the room, as her eyes locked on something that wasn't there. Loralye hoped that she was listening as she continued.

"If he hadn't been sold, if he hadn't been taken away from his father and his family, he would not have been able to accomplish the purpose that God had designed for him to complete. God turns everything that the enemy means for evil into good. I have to believe that is why we are here, and that is why we must endure yet another change."

"So, you think God is going to use us to save some people?" Liz said sarcastically.

Loralye wrapped her arm tightly around her.

"I must believe that Liz. If I don't believe that I am here for a purpose, I don't think that I would make it another day."

"I wish that I could believe in God. I just don't think someone who is supposed to care so much about you would treat you like this."

"Just remember that He didn't do this to you Liz. This all has happened because our world is evil and corrupt. We have free will which means we can decide what we want to believe, and what we are going to do each day. These men who have taken us, they have made some terrible decisions that have affected each of us in the worst way. That doesn't mean that God won't use it for good."

They sat there together for a long while. Loralye stroked Liz's dark hair as Isaiah walked around with Brew. The younger children played with a set of blocks that Porker had found.

Loralye hoped that whatever tomorrow brought, she and her hodge-podge family would see the good that God was planning.

She worried that the choices of her captors were going to be difficult to outshine.

Chapter Thirty-One

The next morning, Loralye helped Liz with the baby carrier. She nestled Brew close to the girl's chest, kissing the top of his head as she wrapped him into the folds.

"Now remember, you take a break as soon as you need to. Sit down and direct Fay and the boys on what to do. They are good helpers."

"I know Miss Loralye, I know. I will make him a bottle when I can't get him to settle, we'll be okay. I will watch him real close, I promise," Liz said as she bounced the now-sleeping baby up and down.

"I know you will. I'm saying everything again for my own comfort, I think. I trust him with you. Thank you, Liz," Loralye said, and she meant it. She did not know how she would have been able to leave Brew with anyone else, bein' that Isaiah was with her.

Porker came a few minutes later with two pieces of paper. "Toby said to give you these Loralye," he said importantly as he handed them to her.

Loralye looked over each of them and then handed the one that had the room assignments to Liz. "Just hold the paper up to the numbers on the door like this," Loralye said as she walked over to the opened door and directed Liz to hold the paper up to the numbers.

"When they match up to a room, that is the one that you need to clean. Porker will help you find them if you can't, won't you Porker" Loralye asked as she looked over at the grown man who was playing tag with James and Fay. It was obvious to her that he was just a boy in a man's body, and she wondered, not for the first time, what his story might be.

He stopped and pretended to shoo away an imaginary fly to hide his embarrassment at his childish behavior. "You know I will. I can't read neither Liz, so don't be embarrassed."

"I'm not embarrassed," Liz said as she straightened her shoulders. "Ain't my fault no one would ever take me to school."

"I will teach you both to read if you want to learn," Loralye said, walking back into the room.

"Do you think I could really learn to read?" Porker asked. The thought of being able to read had always seemed an impossible dream.

"I know you can. We will have our first lesson on Sunday for both of you. Does that sound all right?"

"Does it ever! What would my mama say if she knew her Porker was going to be able to read letters!" Porker did a jig, causing the children to laugh.

"I guess that would be all right," Liz said, begrudgingly.

"I can help too," Isaiah piped in.

"That would be wonderful Isaiah. You would be a big help." Loralye tussled his hair before giving each of the children a big hug.

"Now, you three listen to Liz. It's important that you do a good job today, understand?"

"Yes Miss Loralye," they all replied.

"Let's work on finding another name for you to call me. We are too close for you to be calling me Miss Loralye. Now, go on and get started and we will see you all tonight."

Loralye walked them to the door and watched until they made it to the supply closet.

Looking over the other note she held in her hand, she readied herself for the task ahead. "Are you ready Isaiah?"

"As ready as I'll ever be. I wonder what it's going to be like," he said aloud, but not to anyone in particular.

Porker took the question and answered truthfully. "It ain't gonna be good, that's for sure. Let's get you two over there before I get a call from Toby wonderin' why you ain't got to work yet."

Taking a deep breath, Loralye and Isaiah followed Porker through the tunnel, down the opposite direction. After walking past several doors, Porker pulled out his keys and unlocked a door that looked like all the rest. Loralye was surprised to see stairs that went up on the other side.

For a moment, her heart began to race. Was he leading them out? Just as soon as the thought came, Porker began to give them directions and the hope was snatched away yet again.

"The floor you're heading to is about a ten-minute walk up these stairs. There ain't no other doors up there, so when you get to the one that's up there, just go on in. Someone will be up there waitin' for ya. I'm not sure who's working up today."

"You don't want to come with us?" Isaiah asked.

"Are you kidding me? Do you see all those stairs? I'll keep an eye on the other ones, don't you worry Loralye. Just come on back down when you're done." He pointed to the piece of paper she held tightly in her hand.

"Thank you, Porker, for walking us over here. We will see you tonight."

"Yeah, I'll be here," Porker said before turning around and walking back the way he came, humming a tune.

With a deep breath, Loralye began the assent up the dark hallway with Isaiah following close behind. There was a light every twenty feet or so hanging down the stone wall, illuminating their path. After climbing the long flight of stairs, they made it to the lonesome door.

A light sat to the upper right side of the sea foam metal door. It was dirty, and uninviting. Loralye stood for several moments with her hand on the doorknob, her body, with a mind of its own, seemed unwilling to turn it.

Isaiah came up from behind her and placed his hand over hers. "Let's open it together," he said.

Loralye smiled before they turned the knob together. They pushed the weight of it as one, the heaviness of it surprising them both.

On the other side of the door, there was yet another tunnel, much like the one they had come from. Unsure of what to expect, they both stared down the hall as if unsure what the ground was made of. Loralye didn't know why, but she couldn't make herself take a step in the direction they needed to go.

Isaiah took the first step. "It's okay Miss Loralye, we are going to come up here and do our job, and then we can go back home."

She knew he was right. The thought of getting back to Brew urged her forward. She looked at the paper Porker had given her and read the instructions again. '*Go up the stairs and take the eighth door from the right*' the missive said. They moved onward.

Loralye did not know why she was shaking but decided that her body was already aware of their destination and that somehow, it could sense whatever it was they were about to walk into. As they passed the fifth door, they heard it.

The screams that penetrated the air were unlike anything that Loralye had ever heard before. It was as if an animal was being skinned alive, or a wolf tearing something apart. There were layers on top of each other as though there was more than one person in agony at a time.

Isaiah froze, as Loralye caught up to him. She took his hand in hers, reminding herself that she was the adult here. She had to be the brave one.

"It's okay Isaiah. Let's do as you said and get our work done so we can get back to the others." They took another step.

The screams got louder. Loralye knew that whatever they were about to walk into was going to be hard to stomach, but she took another step. As they passed door six, they were startled, as door seven opened before them.

A man who looked as if he had never before seen the sun, came out of the room holding a tray. Locking the door, he faced the two, obviously not surprised to see them. He was as skinny as a rail, wore glasses, and had stringy, dark, grease-coated hair. His clothes fit loosely on his frame, and his white lab coat was speckled with blood.

He looked up from the tray that held needles and vials filled with a liquid that was unique in color. It was violet. He smiled at Loralye. A gruesome smile. His teeth were blackened with decay.

"Ah, there you are. I have been expecting the two of you. Right this way."

The man walked them past door seven, where the screams were coming from. Loralye gripped Isaiah's hand tighter listening to the shrill screams as they passed the door.

When the man stopped in front of the eighth room, he opened it and walked in.

Isaiah stood still, not wanting to go inside, but this time it was Loralye who pulled on his hand, knowing there was no other choice.

She began to recite one of her favorite scriptures. "The Lord is my shepherd." They took another step. "I shall not want," another. "He maketh me lie down in green pastures; He restores my soul." Then they crossed into the room together.

Isaiah buried his face into Loralye's side when they saw the room. Loralye's hand went up to cover her mouth instinctively, as tears flowed freely from both of their eyes. The man stood by one of the dead children who was hanging by her wrists on one of the walls. He poked her side before turning to face them.

"That one was holding on. A real fighter. Anyways, Toby said that you can get these rooms looking like new. We need to stop the spread of disease as much as possible."

Loralye looked along the walls in horror. Chains hung down every few feet from the ceiling. Shackles lined the walls just below the chains, and blood was caked between the links of each of the rings.

Loralye did her best to appear brave, to appear unmoved, but it was impossible. Her tears continued to flow like a river as Isaiah wailed with compassion for the children who had once filled each of the spaces. She tried to comfort him.

The man looked annoyed but did not say anything. He looked pleased with the contents of his tray and distractedly waved for them to follow him as he walked out of the room and down the hallway. Loralye and Isaiah were each eager to leave the tomb and followed willingly.

They stopped a few doors down at another supply closet. The man cleared his throat and then began talking in a high-pitched, nasally voice that matched his frame perfectly.

"Toby told me what you needed, and I got all the supplies. Just throw the girl in the hall and someone will pick her up later. There is a key next to the door for her restraints, leave it there when you're done. I was told that you have a child down here, and that will be reason enough for you to follow directions. I hope that is the case. You can head back down when you're done."

He started to walk away, leaving them there with so many unanswered questions. Against her better judgment, Loralye called after him. "What are you monsters doing to these poor children down here? How can you live with yourself!" She froze, a few feet outside of the supply closet, as Isaiah stood beside her, obviously afraid of the consequences of her outburst.

The man didn't turn around but stopped in the middle of the hallway. He waved his free hand over each vial on his tray, the liquid shimmering in the light. Without turning around, he said, "Lady, sometimes there is only one choice besides death. To become a part of it." With that reply, he continued to walk away from them, never looking back.

She had so many more questions. She needed to understand how anyone could do these terrible things. What could cause a human being to torture children like this? How could anyone get to the point where they felt that in any way, shape, or form, this was, ok? How could any person be so evil?

Rushing over to door seven, she tried to open it. She pulled and pulled but the lock wouldn't budge. Her mind knew that the door wasn't going to open. She had seen the man lock it. But she had to try. Defeated, she walked back to the supply closet where Isaiah stood waiting.

Loralye worked around him, filling up a bucket with piping hot water and bleach. She grabbed a few rags, a scrub brush, and a mop. Taking a deep breath, she told Isaiah it was time to get to work. Her words brought him out of his stupor, and he moved forward.

As they neared room eight, the woman who carried the weight of so many on her shoulders could be heard whispering under her breath the only comfort she knew. "Yea, though I walk through the valley of the shadow of death, I shall fear no evil." She prayed that the words were still true.

Chapter Thirty-Two

When they finished cleaning the room, both Loralye and Isaiah were completely exhausted. As they walked back down the many stairs to their makeshift family, Loralye's chest ached as her breasts filled with milk. Her shirt was soaked as she leaked through the thin fabric of her worn shirt.

They didn't say anything to each other on the way back. The trauma of the scare room had caused them both to wonder what their reason was to go on living. Was their fate going to bring them to the same chains they had just scrubbed clean? Loralye hoped that was not the case.

She could hear the cries of her child before they entered the room. As they crossed the threshold, she saw Liz bouncing the baby up and down, doing her best to comfort the wailing Brew.

Loralye took the baby from her arms and sat down immediately to feed him. Her milk was ready, and the letdown was strong and quick. She began to sing quietly, doing her best not to wake the three sleeping children on the bed.

After Brew was satisfied and sound asleep, Loralye asked Liz how the day had gone.

"It was hard, but we got everything done. We got finished maybe an hour before you got back."

"How did Brew do? Was he crying this hard all day?" Loralye asked, worried for both Liz and Brew at the thought of having to go through such a traumatic day.

"No, he did well. He took the bottle and slept a lot of the day. He wanted you tonight though. I couldn't comfort him."

Loralye patted his back softly as he slept deeply against her shoulder. She was thankful that he had done better than she had expected. She was also a bit sad though, as the realization that he could make it without her settled in.

How she had missed him that day, and she knew that tomorrow would bring the same feeling of separation. She dreaded it. "I am proud of you Liz, I know that it couldn't have been easy."

Liz shrugged her shoulders as if it were nothing, but Loralye could see that she was pleased with the praise. "How was your day? What was it like," she asked.

Isaiah looked up from where he was sitting, his eyes flashing to Loralye with a look that begged her to be the one to say it. She understood that he was not ready to talk about it, and she wasn't either. Knowing Liz deserved to know some of what they saw, she tried to approach it with as much grace as she could.

"Let's hope you never have to see it, Liz. It isn't good." Pausing, she looked up from Brew and into Liz's eyes. "The horror of that place doesn't compare to anything I have ever seen."

Liz looked across the room at Isaiah. She could see the compassion that had plagued him all day, clearly evident, in his red-rimmed eyes. She didn't ask for any of the details. She could well imagine how awful it was and didn't need to hear the words aloud.

Liz brought over the portion of dinner she had put back for them. The sandwiches and cheese sat next to a canister of water on the small table that Porker had brought in. Loralye took a sandwich and made herself swallow each bite. The bread became gummy in her mouth as if protesting every motion Loralye forced her jaw to make. Every swallow was obligatory, and her stomach echoed its protest.

Isaiah refused to eat. Loralye did not blame him. If it weren't for the need of her baby, she wouldn't have eaten either. She had eaten half of a sandwich and a bite of cheese before giving up on her dinner. Liz packed the rest away for the children the next day.

Exhausted, Loralye fell asleep in the rocking chair as Brew nestled closely against her. Sometime during the night, she was startled awake by the sound of crying. She looked at the baby in her arms, but Brew was still sound asleep. Searching for the source of the pitiful whimpering, Loralye carefully felt around for the flashlight that Porker had given her for emergencies.

Turning on the silver Ray-O-Vac, Loralye found Isaiah curled up in a ball on the floor, his blanket covering his head. She went to him, sat down, and moved Brew to her other arm. Placing the flashlight upright on the ground, she gingerly pulled the threadbare blanket off his head.

"What's wrong Isaiah? You need to sleep. It will be time to go back to work before we know it."

Isaiah wiped his nose, as his tears continued to fall. He sat up and leaned into Loralye, doing his best to stop crying.

. "I just can't sleep Miss Loralye, thinking about what those kids are going through up there. It just doesn't seem right that we are down here with blankets and all, and they are up there. like that.

She knew exactly how he was feeling because she felt the same way. Even though they were prisoners, even though they had been brought to this place against their will, they deserved no better than the children on the scare floor.

"Why should we go clean up the messes those men are making? Why should we help them with what they are doing up there?"

She took a breath, prayed for wisdom, and spoke her heart.

"You know Isaiah, the Bible talks about doing everything as if we are doing it for the Lord. That is hard to know where the line is drawn down here. I will never harm one of those poor souls, and if I get the chance, I will free them. But in the meantime, I am going to do my job and do it well, knowing that the Lord wants me to do my best.

"We also have to remember that what we are doing is helping. If we can keep disease away, if we can keep the smell down, hopefully, we are bringing the children some sort of comfort, even if it's only a little."

"I guess that makes sense. I want to help them as much as I can."

"Me too Isaiah, me too. We also have a few other children down here that we need to take care of for as long as possible," she said as she looked at Liz, Fay, and the two young boys. Yes, they had a few children depending on them, more than they knew.

They sat there for a long while in companionable silence. The glow of the flashlight illuminated the room. Loralye looked from her baby to Isaiah and then to the other four children who were sound asleep on the bed. She knew that she was here for a reason, and she would continue to do her best for each of them.

"Do you think you can sleep for a few hours Isaiah? I know we are going to have an exhausting day tomorrow; I want you well rested."

"I'll try Miss Loralye."

She rubbed his back, comforting him as much as she could. She kissed the top of his head and then said, "Why don't you call me Mama Loralye, would that be okay?"

"Mama Loralye, I like the way that sounds." He smiled shyly. "I didn't think I'd ever have someone to call mama again. Thank you." He wrapped his arms around her, being careful not to disrupt the baby.

Loralye tried to stay strong, tried to remain in control. "Of course, Isaiah. I'm so proud of you. Never think otherwise you hear?"

"Okay mama, I'll try to make you proud every day, no matter what."

"Good boy. Now you go get some rest, I'm going to try and sleep too."

Isaiah wrapped himself back in his blanket, doing his best to fall asleep. Loralye walked tiredly to her bed that lay on the floor. The mattress was thin and worn, but clean. She was thankful that Porker had found another bed for their room. She turned off the flashlight and lay in the darkness, with the baby lying cuddled against her.

Thoughts of the previous day's work began to swarm through her head. She tried to keep them at bay, tried to go back to sleep. Thankful, once again, for the flashlight, she turned it on and ran to the hole they used as a toilet in the corner just in time to empty her stomach of the little amount of food that she had been able to consume.

Isaiah brought over a towel to wipe off her mouth when she was finished. She took it and said thank you. He walked her back to bed and laid down at her feet. Turning off the flashlight for the second time, Loralye sat awake for a long time looking up at the ceiling.

"Mama Loralye, are you still awake?" Isaiah asked, just loud enough to be heard over James's snoring.

"I am."

A little louder he said, "Were you thinking about that finger we found when we were cleaning?"

Loralye took in a sharp breath as bile once again filled her mouth. She answered him honestly. "I was."

"That's what I was thinking about too. It was only a little bit bigger than Brew's."

There was nothing else left to say. They both knew that what they faced was far worse than any monster, than any hate they could have ever imagined. They were caught in the middle of a nightmare and there was no way out.

Chapter Thirty-Three

The next day, Loralye fed Brew, helped the other children get ready for their day of work, and then headed out into the dark stairwell with Isaiah to do their daily tasks.

Porker had brought another missive with breakfast, telling Loralye what was expected to be completed that day. *Room four scrubbed from top to bottom,* she read. She prayed that there were no bodies or parts for them to see this time.

Isaiah was quiet, and she knew that the day was weighing on him just as it was on her. She hummed Amazing Grace as they ascended the staircase. They walked slowly, as if the extra time they spent walking would cause their destination to magically change. It didn't.

When they opened the room, the smell was the first thing that hit their senses. Loralye had seen death, more than she cared to say, but she had never smelled it quite like this. Closing the door, they headed to the supply closet to get what they needed.

The same man they had met the day before passed them on their way back to room four. He was carrying the same tray that she had seen yesterday. The tubes and vials were empty this time. Loralye wondered where the violet liquid came from, and what it was. Her curiosity was aroused.

In his high-pitched nasally voice, the man greeted them like an old friend.

"Well, there you are! I have to say, I didn't know what good you two could do, but that room! Let's just say, I don't mind going in there nearly as much as I used to."

Isaiah clenched his fist, the desire to knock the tray out of the man's hand almost too much for him to resist. Loralye smiled at the man, thinking that maybe this was their ticket to making a difference.

"Well thank you, sir. I'm afraid that I don't know your name. I'm Loralye and this is Isaiah. I am glad that the room meets your standards."

"It sure does, Loralye, I like that name. Someone said your name was Car-something. I can't remember. I guess that doesn't matter since it was wrong anyway. You two keep up the excellent work and we are going to be good friends. My name is Brian. It is good to meet you."

"Brian, what a strong name. It is good to meet you too. I hope that your day is pleasant Brian, we'd best get to work."

"Me too, me too. Good luck in there. Ole Jimmy got a bit carried away." He laughed, as he continued down the hall, disappearing into one of the rooms after he'd unlocked it with his master key.

After they got back inside room four, the duo got to work. Loralye wrapped a rag around both her and Isaiah's mouths and noses to shield them from the smell. It didn't help much. Working their way from top to bottom, they started scrubbing the blood off the walls first.

After they had made it around all four walls, they began cleaning each of the chains. Loralye prayed as she went, hoping that the grace of the Lord would be present with them in the room. They began mopping the floor, and Isaiah guided the liquid toward a drain located in the back of the room.

Urine, feces, and clumps of hair washed down the grates of the drain. Their mop water had to be drained a dozen times before they were finished. Isaiah took the mop and bucket back to the storage closet while Loralye cleaned the larger bits of things that wouldn't go down the drain.

She pushed at a clump of hair with her foot, trying to get it to move its way down the drain. It wouldn't separate, wouldn't mush together, and slide between the small spaces. She carefully picked up the mass with the cloth she had placed on her nose.

As Isaiah walked in, Loralye rushed to hide the glob hidden in the center of the cloth. He looked at her suspiciously because her countenance had changed while he was away.

"Are you okay Mama Loralye? You look spooked."

"I'm fine dear. Is everything put away? Ready to go home?"

He eyed her doubtfully, not completely believing her words. "Yeah, it's put away. Let's go home."

"Yes, let's go."

They walked out of the room. Loralye held tightly to the glob in her hand, doing her best to keep her arm still. When Isaiah opened the door to the stairwell, she unobtrusively threw it down. She would remember to get it tomorrow.

As it rolled to the base of the door, the tiny cloth opened, and the piece of scalp fell onto the floor, the brown hair holding on tightly to the scalloped edges. She hoped someone would have mercy and dispose of it before they came back. She didn't want to touch it again.

The days merged together as they worked on the scare floor. Loralye was able to keep track of time by her days off every Sunday. It had been six months. Brew was rolling over and just starting to sit up. His bulky frame was almost too much for him to hold upright.

Liz continued to grow into a wonderful helper. The children adored her and worked hard under her supervision. Some nights, Brew preferred the company of Liz instead of Loralye, and would whine when kept from her.

Loralye tried not to let it bother her. She knew he spent more time with Liz, and it was only natural that he would want to be with her. James, Fay, and Seth were all doing well, growing in size and in knowledge. James had surpassed Porker in his reading lessons. He was now able to read several scriptures to the group aloud.

Work wasn't any easier, but nothing came as a surprise anymore. Dead bodies were part of the job description. Random body parts would be found, teeth being one of the more common 'parts' to be seen lying on the damp floor.

Loralye and Isaiah had the work down to a science. They could finish cleaning a room from top to bottom in seven hours, which was just long enough to keep them from getting assigned more than one a day.

They would then come downstairs, find Liz and the kids, and help them finish their day's work as well. Loralye loved that she could nurse Brew mid-day and not just during the night.

They tried to play games as they worked. Loralye wanted the children to experience some sort of childhood, she did her best to place as much fun in their path as she could.

After their little church service on Sundays, they would share a meal together. Porker always tried to have something special on Sundays. Today they had brownies along with their chicken soup. The soup was bland, and the brownies were hard, but they all enjoyed them just the same.

After service, they had a reading lesson, followed by singing praise to the Lord together. All the children now called Loralye, Mama. She was amazed that her life had grown to feel so full during the long months of confinement.

Toby had called on Loralye from time to time, his hand never growing softer. She had learned that complying did not mean that you agreed with what was happening. Loralye prayed that she wouldn't become pregnant with his child.

On a day that started like any other, Loralye and Isaiah went to work in room thirteen. They passed several occupied rooms, the screams were excruciating to hear. Isaiah covered his ears as they passed each one, trying to shield himself from the torture that was taking place.

Oddly, they had established some sort of friendship with the man Brian, who never seemed very far away from the screams they heard. He had just exited a room, his tray filled with vials. Loralye noticed that this day, he looked as if he was bothered by the work he had just done. Deciding that there may not be a better moment, she bravely asked him a question.

"Mr. Brian, it's nice to see you today. You don't look so well, "she said, pretending concern. "Is there anything I can do for you?"

He slowed his hand as he locked the room he had just vacated. He held a tray in the other, the vials gleaming in the light, a vibrant violet.

"There is nothing to be done. Some days, things just hit you differently, you know?"

"I'm sure it isn't easy, doing whatever it is they ask you to do in there."

The man turned to face her, and for the first time Loralye saw regret in his pail eyes.

She dared the question, "What is in those vials Brian? What do they get you to do to those children?"

He glanced down at the shining tubes, a forced smile crossing his face. "At first, I enjoyed it. I'm not one to lie. It seemed as if the children were no more than cattle, or livestock. But lately, it doesn't feel the same."

She placed a hand on his shoulder in quiet encouragement to continue. She thought that just maybe her prayers were making a difference. He continued.

"These vials contain something called Adrenochrome. Do you know what that is?" She shook her head no. "It's the fountain of youth they say. I will never have the money to try the stuff, nor would I want to."

"How do they get it?" Loralye asked, as she let her gaze fall to the tray in his hands. Isaiah stood behind her, taking his hands from his ears in order to hear the conversation. The screams never stopped from behind the large door.

Brian looked down each side of the hall, making sure that no one else was around before answering. "They get it from the children. The part that makes it difficult is, they must be terrified before we extract it."

The man looked at her, ashamed, before leaving them alone in the hallway.

Chapter Thirty-Four

Isaiah looked at Loralye just as a shrilling scream erupted from behind the door. He angrily walked away and went to the supply closet. Loralye paused in front of the door. Placing a hand on it, she prayed against a spirit of fear before following Isaiah inside.

When she got to the closet, Isaiah was throwing the assorted cleaning items into a bucket to carry them to room thirteen. After he had all the rags and bleach they would need, he thrust the bucket at Loralye, the force causing her to take a step back in surprise.

He then took a mop bucket and began filling it with warm water. His fury could not overcome his compassion, however, as he wiped angrily at his falling tears. When the bucket was three-fourths full, he grabbed a mop in one hand, the bucket in the other, and stomped into the room.

The room was one of Loralye's least favorites to clean. When they entered room thirteen, they first glanced up at the heavy metal spikes that hung from the ceiling. Isaiah put the bucket on the floor, then grabbed a stool that sat in the corner and climbed it. Loralye handed him a rag to wipe off the spikes. Blood and flesh were dripping from several of them.

When he was ready to move to another section, he threw the rag down, moved his stool, and slammed it against the cold floor. Loralye was unsure how to help him process what they had just learned. They had both had a good idea that this was what was going on, but to hear it spoken out loud made it even more real and horrific.

"Isaiah, it's going to be okay," she said as she handed him the wrung-out cloth.

"How can you say that, Mama? We just learned that little children are being terrified to death, just soes some rich person can look young! How can you say that it's going to be, okay? It sure isn't okay for them!" He cleaned another spike, threw down the cloth, and moved the stool to the next spot.

Loralye didn't know what else she could say. He was right. Things weren't okay. She also knew that she could not allow what was happening on the scare floor to come home with either of them. For the children's sake, they had both decided that the scare floor needed to stay where it was. It had to.

After the spikes were clean, they walked over to the chains that lined both sides of the walls. Loralye counted them every time they went in, hoping there would be less than the time before. Twenty-three; There were still twenty-three spots for children to be shackled and terrified. She was also ready for the Lord to do something.

They finished cleaning the room, and Isaiah's attitude only grew worse. His anger threatened to overtake him when he had to pull out a small bone that had gotten lodged in the drain. They weren't sure what body part it was from.

After they had put everything away, they walked back down the long staircase to help the others. Loralye hoped that he would be able to keep what they had learned to himself. There was no need to instill more fear in the others than they already had.

Porker met them at the bottom of the staircase. He walked them to where Liz was waiting with the children. "You okay Isaiah? Something ain't right with you."

Isaiah clenched his jaw but didn't say anything. Loralye reached for his hand, but he jerked it away. She sighed and spoke on his behalf. "It was a hard day today, Porker, that's all."

Porker left it alone. She was thankful for that. He began to tell Loralye how he had *almost* won a game of cards the night before. Pride radiated from him.

"Very well-done Porker, maybe you will win next time."

He looped his fingers around his suspenders, nodding his head. "I bet I will! I just got to save up some extra cash so I can get in the pot again. Payday is coming up. We'll see if they gots the gusto to beat Ole Porker again."

Loralye hoped that they were not cheating this simple-minded man that they had all grown to love. As they opened the door where the children were working, the group rushed over to see them. Little Brew began to kick his legs excitedly, as Liz worked as quickly as she could to get him untangled from the carrier, she had held him in while she worked.

"Hold on little guy, I'll get you to Mama as fast as I can," Liz said as she laughed at his obvious joy.

Loralye took him gladly. Holding him closer, she blew bubbles on his neck, causing Brew to laugh aloud. Taking a break from their work, the other children congregated around the laughing baby, Porker, Loralye, and Isaiah. James wrapped his arms around Porker for a hug and then went over to hug Isaiah. Isaiah shrugged out of his hold and left the circle that they had created. Loralye saw the hurt in James's eyes. Isaiah had never treated him that way before.

Seeing his hurt and confusion, Loralye went to him. Isaiah had a hard day today, little one. Don't take it personal, okay?"

"Okay Mama, I won't." He smiled innocently before going back to where Porker stood to hear him tell everyone how he had almost won at cards.

They finished their list of rooms together before returning home for dinner. Porker had started eating with them every night a few months back, which was good for several reasons.

The first was the laughter that Porker brought with him. He could tell a story about walking to the bathroom that would have you rolling on the floor. The second reason was since he was eating whatever the group was being fed, their meals had gotten substantially better in flavor and size.

As they ate the roast beef sandwiches and apples, Loralye looked over at the bed where Isaiah had chosen to sit. Normally he would be at the table with them, enjoying the company and food together. Today, not only was he alone, but he also refused to eat.

Loralye knew she was going to have to talk with him. She was unsure of what she could say, unsure of what the right answer should be in this situation. Of course, these children needed their help. But if they helped them, they would, at the same time, be handing over the children she loved as her own to the evil vices of that place.

Loralye would have to pray about what to do. Her flesh told her that doing nothing was the right option, but watching Isaiah stare hopelessly up at the ceiling, let her know that doing nothing might be the easier option, but it was not the right one. They were going to have to do something to try and change the fate of the children.

After Porker had left and the other children fell asleep, Loralye walked over to talk to Isaiah. Staring up at the ceiling, he looked at her for a moment before going back to staring at the smooth surface. "What do you want Loralye," he said.

The words hurt more than she could say. Isaiah hadn't called her that in a long while. She tried not to take it personally, knowing that the boy was hurting as well. She sat down on his bed and prayed for strength.

"Isaiah today was hard for me too. I know that you want to do something, but we aren't ready to help them yet."

He turned over onto his side to face her. "So what? You think we need to just keep doing everything they tell us to do? We need to keep scrubbing the blood and guts off the walls so they can just do it again the next day? I'm tired of it! I would rather be one of the ones on those chains than help them in their evil ways."

James squirmed in his sleep, the volume of Isaiah's voice nearly waking him. When he stilled, Loralye quietly replied.

"I know how you feel, I feel that way too sometimes." He harrumphed, not believing her. Loralye went on. "Isaiah, I know that it doesn't seem like it, but I have been praying that God would set up a divine intervention for us to help. We must remember though, that His timing is perfect. If we try to free them before it's time, we may not succeed."

He seemed to be listening, Loralye's words settling within him. She went on, "Our first priorities are to these sweet little ones we have been given charge of. What would happen to James, Fay, Peter, and Brew? To Liz? She is right at the age where they would take her to the Residence and we both know that would finish her."

Isaiah closed his eyes, realizing that she was telling the truth. He let it settle in. "It just all feels so pointless. I want to help set them free and there just isn't anything I can do to help."

"You are helping!"

"Loralye, making sure it smells better isn't my definition of helping. Sure, it might be one less thing they have to deal with, but I highly doubt the kids are chained up there thinking, wow, it smells good in here."

Loralye took a deep breath, Isaiah's frustrations causing her to question everything. She sat there for a while, waiting for the Lord to guide her words. Knowing King David was Isaiah's favorite, she decided to use the story from the bible to demonstrate her point.

"Did you know King David was anointed to be King years before he actually became king?" She had his attention. "What if David had gotten anointed and then just walked over to the throne and demanded to have it right then and there? Would that have worked well for him?"

"No."

"Right! They would have laughed in his face and possibly killed him for coming against the King. If that would have happened, all the good he had accomplished would never have happened."

She laid down next to Isaiah, forcing her arm around him. He finally gave in and put his weight on her shoulder.

"Just because you feel that you have been anointed to protect these children, does not mean that the time is yet appointed. We must wait for the right timing Isaiah, or we could ruin everything the Lord is doing here."

He wrapped his arm around Loralye in a hug. "I'm sorry for how I treated you today, Mama."

"It's okay Isaiah, I understand the turmoil you feel inside. It hits me too at times. You have no idea how hard it is to put your hands to something like this, knowing your baby could face the same consequences if you fail. At times, it feels hopeless. We just need to remember who our enemy is. It should never be against each other."

"I know, I know."

They sat there together, leaning on one another for comfort. Isaiah finally began to drift in and out of sleep. Right before he gave in to a deep slumber, he said, "But how will we know when it's time? When we are ready?"

Loralye pulled him closer. She said with a confidence she did not know she had. "I prayed that the Lord would give us a key. When it comes, it will be time."

Chapter Thirty-Five

---◇---

New York, New York, Two Days until infiltration

Kay came home from work completely drained. Working all day as Governor, and then coming home and working on Operation Exodius, (as they had so aptly named it), was wearing her down. Carter wanted to force her to rest, but he knew that it would be pointless. Even if he could convince her to lie down, there was no way she would be able to go to sleep.

Since he knew sleeping was not an option, Carter planned to go completely in the opposite direction. Instead of helping her sleep, he would help her stay awake. Two carafes of coffee sat on the dining room table, fresh and full. He'd had that and an assortment of baked goods delivered from 'Hebrews, She Bakes'. Muffins, cookies, and scones surrounded the table, and the familiar smell of baked goods and coffee was comforting.

"This is wonderful. Thank you, Babe," Kay said, as she wrapped her arms around Carter and kissed him.

"Hey now you two, if I need to go home for a bit, please let me know. I am too old for all of that," Al said, as he walked around the couple heading for the table of deliciousness.

Kay slowly pulled away, giving Carter one more peck on the cheek before following Al.

"Now don't take all the blueberry scones this time, those are my favorite."

"They are my favorite too," Al said, pouting.

Carter laughed and walked towards the large oak table. "I bought extra scones you two! There will be no fighting, you hear me?"

They laughed, got a coffee and pastry, and went back upstairs to the office to continue working. "I can't believe we only have two days left," Kay said in a rare moment of vulnerability.

"We can do a lot in two days," Al said, always the eternal optimist. "Operation Exodius is going to change the nation, I can feel it."

"I hope you're right. We still need to get all these entry points covered. How is that list coming?"

Al drained his coffee before getting up and walking to the map they had pinned to the wall. They had red pins on the entries they still needed covered, and green ones on the areas where they had teams ready to go. There had to be close to a hundred green pins, but even more red ones littered the map.

"We aren't even sure if all of these are still entrances, Kay. If we find that they are not being used, the teams will move to the next nearest site. I have tried to get at least one team in every state, but we are running out of time to find enough teams to get to the further locations. That guy I told you about from the special opts team has thirty guys he has rounded up going to Texas right now. They are going to get there just in time."

"I know you're right, it just makes me uneasy. What if we pick the wrong ones? What if they get away again?"

"We are going to get them Kay, I can feel it." Al walked over to the window, the excitement of the mission invigorating him.

Pulling him away from his thoughts and back on their conversation, Carter said, "Al, tell Kay about the MCP teams you have."

"MCP?" Kay asked.

"That's what we started calling the Missing Children Parent Teams. It's easier," Al shrugged. "You're not going to believe it. We have over fifty dads who have stepped up. I made it as clear as I could that the probability of them finding their children is extremely low, but every one of them is still harboring hope. I can't blame them, I would too."

"As would I," Kay said. "But that is incredible. They are definitely motivated to do whatever they can to get inside of there. We are just going to have to hope that they won't make any mistakes in their excitement."

"That is why I decided to place them as the lookouts for the trained teams I have going in. They are going to stand back, close to where we have the video footage, and wait for a signal to go in on the radio. If they do not get the signal, they have been instructed to stand down."

"That's a good idea. How amazing would it be if we ended up finding some of their lost children?"

"I think that would be the icing on the cake. I have been praying that families would be reunited through all this," Al said.

"Me too. Well, what do we need to finish today? I took the next two days off work so that we can run at this with everything we have."

"I don't have anything else to do right now. We are waiting for the cameras to be set up, and then we can get everything connected to the monitors I have set up in the warehouse. We will be able to watch every team as they attempt to enter the various locations."

Kay sat down in her office chair and picked up her phone. "Well, I am going to take that as an okay to call Saul and have him bring Hope home for the evening then. He was going to keep her while we worked, but I would love to see her if we are in a waiting game."

"That sounds like a great idea. I wouldn't mind seeing her myself." Al left the office and headed back downstairs to get another cup of coffee.

Carter went around the desk and stood behind Kay. He rubbed her shoulders as she talked to her brother. When she got off the phone, he turned her around in the chair to face him. He smiled, put his hand on her cheek, and told her how proud he was of her.

"I haven't accomplished much yet. Maybe you should save that line for later."

"I mean it, Kay. You are a wonderful mother, the best Governor this state has seen in years, an amazing wife, and you are about to save hundreds, maybe thousands of children. I couldn't be prouder of you."

"I couldn't do any of this without you Carter."

He pulled her up and held her close. "I have a feeling you would have figured it out."

"You have too much faith in me."

"I have faith in the One who is in you, my love. Jesus decided to use you a long time ago. He didn't need me to be here to make sure it would happen, but I sure am glad that He decided to let me come along for the ride."

Kay squeezed him tighter. "Me too my love, me too."

The next day, Kay spent extra time getting Hope up and ready. She wouldn't get to see her again until this was all over. As Hope drank her morning bottle, Kay read her their favorite book *The Gruffalo*. After she was dressed in one of her cutest outfits, she packed her bag for the few days she would be spending away from home. Soon afterward, Solomon picked her up, Lailey sitting excitedly in the car seat right beside Hopes in the back.

"We are going to have so much fun Aunt Kay! I have all my stuffed animals lined up in the living room, and I'm going to show Hope each one! Then, we are going to play house, watch a movie, and draw pictures."

Kay and Carter looked at baby Hope who was sound asleep in her car seat, knowing she would not have half as much fun as Lailey was going to. They both smiled at the little girl's enthusiasm.

"I hope you two have so much fun Lailey! We will see you both in a few days. You help keep an eye on her, okay?"

"I will!"

They each gave Hope one last kiss before watching the car back out of the driveway.

"You ready for this?" Carter asked.

"I think I have been ready for this for the past thirty years."

Hand in hand, they walked inside where Al was waiting.

"You guys ready to head over to the warehouse?"

"We are. Let's get going."

They drove together to the building the Wyleys had rented a few months back. It wasn't anything fancy, but it was close to Central Park, and it was big enough to house a lot of people short term, which was exactly what they needed. It also didn't stand out, which was a plus.

Al pulled the unmarked car into the back of the building, where a loading dock was open and ready for them. After he pulled in, the large metal door closed behind them. It took a moment for Kay's eyes to adjust from the bright sunlight to the dim warehouse shadows.

When she could focus, she was amazed at what she saw. Dozens of monitors lined the far wall, and many people were working at computer stations scattered across the room. Most of them were women wearing black headsets that connected them to the various rescue teams around the country.

Tears came to Kay's eyes as she saw each person working diligently, hitting buttons, and answering questions that they were receiving on their headsets.

"Where did you find all of these people Al?" she asked in a hushed tone. She knew that he had found hundreds to help but seeing it in person was mind-blowing.

"These Kay, these are mothers of the lost."

Kay walked over and shook each mother's hand. She still could not believe Al had put this together in six short days. Carter followed close behind, stopping to ask questions as little red dots began to flash on the screens.

"When they are red, that means the cameras are set up. We can click on them, and it pulls up the footage," one of the women said.

She demonstrated by clicking on one of the red markers. It brought up one of the possible entrances on one of the large monitors. On the screen, they saw a little house in the middle of nowhere, run down and dilapidated.

"Where are the cameras located? Are they hidden well?" Kay asked.

"You'd never know they were there Kay," Al said, joining them from behind.

"We ordered several that look like stones. Some we attached to car tires and parked them across from the entrances. Others look just like tree bark. I suppose that a few may be detected, but my guess is, we will be pleasantly surprised with the technology."

"And how does the footage get back here?"

"Wi-Fi. We set each team up with a hot spot. They are all close to their entrances, ready to go when I give the signal."

"It's amazing," Carter said, pointing to several red marks as the women switched between them.

"It gets better. Carol, click on team one-eleven please."

"You got it," Carol said. She quickly found the camera Al was wanting, pulled it up on the screen, and then hit a button on her keyboard.

Through the speakers, they heard, "One-eleven here, ready to move at your command."

Al walked to the microphone and responded. "Just checking in one-eleven. Any activity?"

"We saw a man go in an hour ago. He was holding something we couldn't identify. It took all I had not to follow."

"Roger that, one-eleven. Keep your cool out there. We need to follow the plan, copy?"

"Copy that sir. We are ready and waiting for Operation Exodius to begin."

"Over and out."

"Wow! That is cool," Carter said, walking towards the microphone.

"Don't even think about it," Al said as he moved the mic away from Carter's grasp.

"Come on Al, can't I talk some lingo with one team?"

"Absolutely not."

Kay laughed at the two men as they bantered back and forth about using the microphone. Carol pulled out another chair for her and showed her how to navigate the system that Al had set up.

"Thank you so much for helping with this Carol, I just can't get over how many people have given their time for this."

Carol sat back in her chair, pulling her eyes away from the giant screen and focusing on Kay. "I would spend the rest of my life for one more day with my daughter, April. She was taken right out of our home thirteen years ago. She was only two."

"I am so sorry Carol, I can't imagine."

"I've heard your story, Ms. Mayor. I figure you can imagine better than most. I hope that by helping, we will make a difference in at least one family's future. I know I would be forever grateful if it changed mine." She turned back to the computer and continued checking in on the various teams.

Kay prayed that tomorrow would change the stories of more families than she could ever imagine. She prayed that tomorrow would begin the Exodus of the lost.

Chapter Thirty-Six

The next morning, Kay pulled on her boots over her long socks. She looked in the mirror, and for the first time in a long time, did not mind what she saw. She wasn't wearing her designer clothes and hadn't seen Sky for a hair appointment in a while. Grays were beginning to pop through, but it didn't bother her.

She had on a long-sleeved black shirt with a bulletproof vest fastened over it, courtesy of Al. Cargo khaki pants finished the look. She had a few wrinkles and could stand losing those five pounds she had gained over the last year, but for the first time, maybe ever, it wasn't what she saw on the outside that she was looking at.

She was, for the first time in her life, feeling as if she had done something right. It was as if there was an inner light shining through. It wasn't what the world saw that mattered. It was what she saw, what she was working towards. She was grateful that God had called her to this important work, and it fulfilled her like nothing else could.

Walking out of the women's restroom, she met Carter in the hallway. Unaware that she was there, Carter was pacing back and forth, waiting for Kay. She had forgotten how handsome he was in uniform. His brown army pants were tucked into his tan combat boots which matched his tan, form-fitting tee. His bulletproof vest rested over his shoulders.

When he saw Kay, he walked towards her, his eyes taking in her every inch. He turned his finger in a circle, and she obliged by slowly twirling in the muted light of the warehouse. "Stunning."

She went to him. He ran his hands through her hair, and she was glad she had waited to put it up.

"This brings back a lot of memories, doesn't it?" Kay asked, her body tingling as he ran his hand down her back.

"It sure does. I know you love your designer clothes and workout attire, but I think I'm going to make it mandatory that you wear something like this at least once a month."

"You look good too babe."

They stood there, holding each other for a few long moments. They both knew that the next few hours were critical. This was either going to bring this nightmare to an end, or it had been all for nothing.

"What if Andrea was wrong? What if these entrances are really nothing? What if we have been scoping out old parks and buildings and that's all they are?"

"We can't think like that love, and we don't need to. Let's trust that the Lord brought us to this moment on purpose. That the lady in the diner, the man with the journal that brought us to Lilah and Hope, the tragedy of you being taken from your family at such an early age was all for a purpose."

"Okay, I know you are right. I will try not to freak out for at least five minutes when we start this."

"How about ten minutes?"

"Deal."

He pushed the hair out of her face, taking in every inch of her one last time before heading out to his post at Central Park.

"Now, when I come back with dozens of children in tow, and bad guys handcuffed together, I expect you to be proud of me."

227

She kissed him soundly, trying not to let the tears fall. "Carter, I have been proud of you every single day that I have known you. I would never have been able to do this without your support. You are my greatest treasure."

"And you, are mine."

"You come back to me now, you hear?"

"I will, don't you worry. Al set this team up with more men than we could ever need. I think he's worried I'm going to get into trouble."

"You're sure you don't want to stay and help navigate here in the warehouse? We could use you here too, you know?"

He wrapped his arm around Kay, holding her close one more time. "I was trained for this Kay. I'll be safe, I promise. Besides, you know Al, he will be telling me on the radio what to do every step of the way. He's not going to let me get into a situation I can't get out of."

She knew he was right. Reluctantly, she let him go. They walked together to the main room where all the monitors were set up. Carter called everyone together for a word of prayer before they put Operation Exodius into motion.

"Father, we don't believe it is by accident that You have brought us all together. Even as we go out in our separate teams, we have the same mission. I pray that You would go before us. That doors would be opened that have been shut for far too long, that You would bring to light what has been going on in the darkness for to many years."

"We pray that you would protect the teams that have put their lives on the line and that no child would be hurt in our extractions. Above all Lord, we pray that Your will be done. In His name, Amen."

"Amen," was echoed by the group.

Carter squeezed Kay's hand tight before leaving with his team to head down the block to Central Park. Pulling herself together, Kay took her place beside Carol. They gave the fifteen-minute call to all the teams. It was almost time. Al put his headset on and handed Kay hers.

"Are you ready?" He asked.

"As ready as I ever am going to be."

Al took the microphone and instructed Carol to broadcast to every team. Holding down the button on the transmitter, he gave the command. "Operation Exodius underway. Teams, let's move!"

Carol began to flip from one camera to the next. They watched as the different teams began knocking down doors, opening manholes in the middle of the road, and moving brush away beside old buildings.

They all waited for someone to come back with a sign of something, but so far, nothing. Carol put Carter's team on one of the monitors and left it there as she switched between the others on another screen. Kay's heart pounded as she watched her husband disappear behind a large oak tree.

Five minutes later, still nothing. Kay was beginning to lose heart. "Lord, please let this be it, let us get to them, please." Kay prayed silently, fervently.

Carol jumped to a location that looked like it was in the middle of a desert, no movement. She switched to one that had a park in the background, nothing. Al went to grab the radio to talk to some of the MCP teams. Just before he could hit the button, they saw something.

"Switch back to that last channel Carol," He asked, his voice excited. Carol went back to the last location with the touch of a button. They saw the MCP's running towards the entrance in a rush, they had found something.

Chapter Thirty-Seven

Underground, 1968, Four years later

Loralye finished passing out breakfast, while Liz poured her and Isaiah a cup of coffee.

"Thank you dear, this is exactly what I needed for today. Room thirteen is always a hard one."

Liz gave her a hug. "The day will be over before you know it, Mama. Are we going to read on in Psalms tonight?"

"I would like to. I still can't believe Porker found us another Bible. How wonderful is it to be able to read together, bouncing back and forth?"

"I love it. It helps me to soak it in when I can follow along with you. I'm hoping he will be able to get one for each of us. Fay talks about it constantly."

"Oh, that would be such a blessing. I will pray he does."

Their attention was captured by Brew who began crying hard at something one of the others had said, a spoon of oatmeal in his hand uneaten.

"What on earth could have you crying so hard this early in the morning?" Loralye asked as she kissed him on the cheek.

"James said Isaiah and Liz are gonna get married, Mama!" He wrapped his arms around her, and Loralye cringed as she felt the spoon of oatmeal slide down her back. Doing her best to ignore it, she scooped Brew up and walked him over to her bed.

She held him as he sniffled, and the others looked over in concern. She smiled at them, each one going back to their previous tasks. Loralye rubbed her son's back, doing her best to comfort him. She wondered how many more days she would be able to hold him like this. He was a big boy, and his size was quickly overtaking her own.

When the tears had finally stopped, he raised his head off her chest. "Mama, if Liz marries Isaiah, who am I going to marry? I don't wike Fay"

Loralye was surprised at how soon her son had understood the concept of having a spouse. She had told countless stories of her and Abe, and she wondered if she had overly romanticized it. She took the spoon out of his hand and placed it on the ground next to her worn shoes.

"Now Brew, we have talked about this before. You will marry whomever the Lord has for you. It may be Fay; it may be someone we haven't met yet. What is important is that it's who He wants for you, not who you want for yourself.

"You're not ready to get married, are you? You do look taller than yesterday, but I am certain you didn't have another birthday last night, did you?"

He shook his head. "No mama, my birthday is still a few momfs away."

"Yes, that's what I thought. Now, Isaiah and Liz might get married, or they might not. But if that's what the good Lord has for them, that's what we should want too, right?"

"Yes, Mama."

"That's my good boy. You have a long time until you need to think about getting married, don't worry about it right now love. You go on and finish breakfast. It's almost time to go to work." Brew kissed her cheek before running over to the table.

She looked over to Liz and Isaiah who were standing by the door talking. How had she not seen the attraction building between them before? She thought that they very well might get married. They were definitely smitten with one another.

Her thoughts were interrupted when Porker came with the day's assignment like he did most every morning. What little hair he had left was beginning to gray. Loralye wondered if everyone who worked down in the tunnels aged as quickly as he had.

He went over to Brew and handed him a small bouncy ball. The boy was thrilled. Peter, Fay, and James all watched as Brew chased around the blue ball that wouldn't stay still. The joy of the room blessed Loralye's heart to nearly overflowing.

As she and Isaiah prepared to go upstairs, they bid farewell to each of them. Porker led the way to the rooms they had been assigned for the day. Liz stayed behind to spend a few more moments with Isaiah. Loralye walked a little of the way with Brew, giving the two a rare few moments of privacy.

She held his not-so-little hand in hers as he skipped along with his little blue ball in his other hand. She laughed with him as they neared their destination. When they got to the crew's first room, James, Fay, and Peter went to the supply closet to get what they needed for the day. Loralye looked at her son again, her eyes watering.

"Why are you looking at me like that Mama?"

"Oh, no reason Brew. You just remind me an awful lot of your father."

"Was he big like me?"

"You know he was! He had to duck down when he went into most places. Your daddy was tall and had so many muscles, just like you."

Brew stood a little straighter at the mention of muscles, and she suppressed a laugh. He put his ball into his pocket and then wrapped his arms around Loralye's waist.

"I wish I got to meet him."

"So do I Brew, so do I. He would have been so proud of you, do you know that?"

"You told me."

"Well, I don't want you to ever forget it. We both are so proud of the man of God you are becoming."

"I'm proud of you too Mama."

"For what?"

"You try so hard to keep us happy, and you make me smile every day. You work hard too. Maybe tonight we can play with my ball together?"

"I would love that. You go along now and listen to Liz. I love you my little cup of Brew."

Brew smiled at the nickname she had given him. She bent down to hug him, kissing his cheek before retracing her steps back towards Isaiah and Liz.

Loralye cleared her throat when she saw the two kissing in the hallway. Liz blushed and quickly pulled away. Retreating towards the children, her smile could have lit a hundred rooms. Isaiah watched her walk away, his hands finding his pockets.

Loralye passed him and headed to the staircase. Isaiah reluctantly followed. His mood lifted. "Mama, Liz is the one. I just know it."

"I think you may be right son."

"Do I have your blessing to marry her? I know we don't have a pastor down here, so I thought maybe you could do it."

"Let me pray about it and get back to you. This all seems very sudden."

"I guess that's fair. I just don't want to wait. I love her. I have for a long time. I just didn't say it aloud. I was afraid she wouldn't feel the same way. Lucky me, she does."

"How do you know she's the one?" Loralye asked as they continued up the dark staircase.

"I just know. When she is around, she's all I can think about. When she isn't around, I can't stop wishing that she was. She loves the Lord and is a hard worker. She is so good with the others, and I just, I don't know. I don't want to be without her."

"You're a little young to be getting married, don't you think?"

"I don't know, maybe I am. It just seems like the next step in my life. If this is going to be my forever, I want to do it with her by my side."

"I think if we could wait a few more years, that might be more appropriate."

"Did you say years? Oh, Mama, I don't want to wait that long. Please pray about it and see what the Lord says. I will take care of her; I believe she is my other half. If we weren't stuck down here, I think I would have found her anyway. I'm sure she's the one." He put his hand over his heart. "We were made for each other."

Loralye didn't say anything else. Her heart was glad. She remembered meeting Abe and how quickly she had known that he was her match. There was no pushing the feelings down. Now she just needed to pray for when the Lord wanted the union to take place. Her children were growing up.

When they entered the scare floor, something was different. Loralye opened the door and was dumbfounded. In the middle of the hallway, Brian sat with a small, lifeless girl in his arms. She was covered in blood, her veins bruised from the extractions they had made.

When her senses came to her, Loralye rushed to them. Unsure how to help, she carefully took the girl out of his arms. She was still warm to the touch. Loralye checked for a heartbeat, but there wasn't one. Isaiah joined them, kneeling, he carefully took the girl from Loralye's arms and took her to the incinerator.

He hated that part of the job. As he had gotten older and stronger, they had forced the task on him. Isaiah knew that if he wanted to stay with Mama and Liz, he had to do what he was told. He decided he would rather be forced to help clean up after the monsters than be made into one of them. He always said a prayer before he said goodbye to them forever.

Loralye's heart hurt every time she had to watch him take one of the lifeless bodies away. She looked back at Brian, his silence concerning. "What happened in there Brian?" She asked.

He sat there on the floor, motionless. He stared at the wall with his eyes glazed over. Isaiah had made it back to them before Brian spoke.

"The little girl you just took away, her name was Sarah." He paused, and his breathing began to speed up. He looked at Loralye, his eyes portraying more than words.

"I was coming in after a session to collect the Adrenochrome. All the others were the same as any other, they screamed as I extracted the substance from them. Then I got to Sarah. She wasn't scared Loralye, not at all."

"What do you mean she wasn't scared?"

"I mean, everything the guys tried to do, didn't cause her pulse to go up like we needed, didn't cause the fear we needed to extract from her." He got on his knees and moved closer to the woman who had become a good friend.

Taking her hands into his, he started to cry. "She told me, she told me that she forgave me for what I was doing to her. That it wasn't my fault I had such a mean heart. That God would forgive me too if I asked Him to, just like you have told me all these years."

"I had hurt her Loralye. I had beaten her and done things that should never happen to a child. And then, she forgave me."

The man began to cry. Loralye took him into her arms, thanking God for the compassion he had shown to this broken man. She also thanked the Lord for the little girl who had, at some point in her life, met God in a tangible way. What a brave little one she was.

Isaiah stood there, unsure how to move forward. They were in front of the room they were to clean that day, room thirteen. Brian pulled away from her, wiping his snotty face off in his shirt. Isaiah said, "I guess we should get to work."

Brian stood up quickly, fear causing him to look all around.

"What is it, Brian," Loralye asked.

"I couldn't do it Loralye, couldn't go through with it. I can't do this anymore." He pulled her hand over to him, opened it, and placed something inside of it before running away. After the door slammed, Isaiah asked Loralye, "What is it?"

Loralye opened her fist and showed him what had been placed in her care. There, in her hand, was Brian's master key.

Chapter Thirty-Eight

New York, New York, Present Day

Kay stood and began pacing the room. They were waiting for someone, anyone to tell them what was going on. Carol went from team to team, listening to the mics. They couldn't hear anyone.

"Al, where is everyone? Why can't we hear them?"

Al clicked between monitors, watching the screens, and waiting for some of the men to reappear. Several of them were gone.

"Kay, I'm wondering if they are too far underground to have a signal, or, if there is a disturbance in the tunnels to jam the signals. I can't believe we overlooked this!"

Kay brought her gaze back up to the monitor of Central Park. Carter was still out of sight.

"I'm going out there to check on Carter." Kay grabbed her jacket from the back of the chair and threw it on.

"There is no way I am letting you go, Kay," Al said.

"I'm going. If you want to protect me, you better get moving. You forget that I have been trained for this kind of work Al"

"Carter is not going to be happy about this," Al said as he stood up, chambered a round, and put his gun back in his holster.

"Don't worry, he will know whose idea it was. Let's get going."

"Carol, you radio in if you hear or see anything. Kay and I will be on channel 17."

"You got it boss, be careful."

He paused for a moment before following behind Kay. When they exited the building with two more guards in tow, Kay smiled to herself. "I think you may have an admirer there, Al."

Al passed her with a jog, taking the lead toward Central Park. "Why don't you let me worry about that? One assignment at a time. Let's go!"

The team picked up its pace and headed towards the entrance behind the large oak tree. Kay looked back over her shoulder one last time, wondering if Carol was watching. Stepping past the brush that surrounded the trunk, Kay and the others ran out of sight.

Underground, 1968

Loralye looked at Isaiah, his eyes wild with panic. Loralye got up from the ground and gripped her fingers over the key. "We have been praying for this moment Isaiah, I just didn't think it was going to be today."

"Neither did I," he said.

She looked at the boy who had become a man far too quickly. Thinking over the nearly five years they had had together, Loralye's heart ached at what she had to do.

"Do you trust me, Isaiah?"

Isaiah looked at her with sorrow, moisture began to pool in both his eyes, causing Loralye to let hers flow as well. "Of course, I trust you, Mama."

"Good. I am so proud of you Isaiah. Now, I need you to listen, and I need you to listen well. You are going to go downstairs to Toby's office and tell him that you want to talk to him about something important, I am not sure what, you're going to have to think of something."

"No Mama."

"Don't you tell me no son; this is for your own good. You try to spend as much time as you can with him. Then, when you get back here, you run and tell Porker that I'm gone. You run to him and make it sound urgent, you hear?"

"Mama," Isaiah cried harder.

"Now you stop those tears right now! You can't have your eyes all red when you go to Toby." She wiped off his face, leaving her hand on his cheek for one last moment.

"You tell Liz that I saw her Mama's heart the first time I laid eyes on her."

"Mama."

"You tell the boys and Fay that they need to keep working hard, and they need to read their Bible every single day. Don't let one day go by without them reading it son, you hear me?"

"I can't do this Mama, I can't leave you up here." Isaiah cried harder.

As if to cement her plan into place, they heard a scream behind door thirteen that was enough to make your skin crawl. Loralye closed her eyes as she spoke her final words to Isaiah.

"You tell Brew that I love him ever so much. You tell him to grow up to be just like his daddy, a protector for the ones who can't protect themselves.

"You must go protect our family, Isaiah. We have prayed for a key, and here it is. I must do something. Your job here on out is to protect those children. Protect Brew for me. Promise me, Isaiah!"

Isaiah wiped at his tears one last time before hugging Loralye and kissing her on the cheek. "I promise Mama, I promise."

"You're going to be a mighty fine husband to that girl Isaiah, mighty fine."

"Thank you, Mama."

She squeezed him hard, then motioned him towards the door at the far end of the long hallway. She waited for the door to close before placing the key in the lock of room thirteen. She took a deep breath, turned it, and heard the door click open.

Chapter Thirty-Nine

New York, New York, Present Day

Al and Kay walked up to the back of the tree which was wide open. "How did they do this?" She asked no one in particular.

"We will worry about that later. You two, you go in first. Kay, you follow me. There is absolutely no going around me, do you copy?"

"I copy Al, I copy."

"All right then, let's move!"

The two men ran in front of Al and started climbing down the stairs that were hidden by the large tree right in the middle of the park. Motion sensory lights began to light up as they went every few steps. Al took a headlamp out of his vest and put it on just in case they lost the lighting. The stairs went on and on. Kay wondered how far underground they were. Al tried to reconnect with Carol, but they didn't have a signal.

"I'm not surprised we can't reach headquarters. We have got to be several hundred feet underground." He placed his hand on the side of the wall. "Feels like concrete. That would block the signal quite a way back."

They continued working their way down the steep staircase, the walls growing a little closer together with every few steps. Just when Kay thought she would have to stop and rest for a minute, they saw a landing.

The two guards ran into the opening, with their guns out and ready. Al stood at the entrance, gun pointed in his right hand, his other holding Kay back. When he saw that there was no danger, he motioned for her to follow.

The room they entered was dark and dome-like in shape. There was an old desk behind a counter that looked as if it hadn't been used in years. Tables sat to the right with old clothes piled on top of them. Kay went over to one and held up, it couldn't be for a child over the age of five.

Dust covered her hand as she placed the shirt back on top of the pile. Al called for her to catch up and she did. They entered a long tunnel that had doors on each side, much like the ones they had found when they rescued Lilah. They were all empty.

The team ran on, and Kay began to worry about Carter. Where was he? Al tried the radio again, but still no signal.

"Quick, over here!" One of the men called from the front of the line.

As Kay passed the door with the shot-off lock, they took a sharp right. The lights continued to turn on as they continued. Kay looked back and could see the darkness closing in behind them as the motion-censored lights began to shut off.

After a few more minutes of jogging, they saw a light far into the distance that had not been turned on by them. She could see movement, it was Carter. Kay pressed on, her side beginning to ache at the tempo they had kept.

When they finally reached them, Carter looked up and smiled. Sitting on the floor were two men handcuffed and gagged.

"I couldn't stand to hear the filth coming out of their mouths. Kay, we did it." Carter pointed towards the room to his right.

Kay walked over and peered inside. There, sitting in a dozen different beds, was the first group of missing children.

Underground, 1968

Loralye took a deep breath and went inside. Running towards the screaming child, she took her key and quickly unlocked the girl's shackles. "It's okay love, I'm not going to hurt you."

The girl went limp in her arms. She had passed out. Loralye put her gently on the ground and then went to the next set of chains. A little boy hung lifeless by his wrists; a weapon dangled from the top of his arm. Loralye released his restraints and put him on the ground next to the tray Brian had left. She crossed his arms and closed his eyes for the last time.

"May you find peace at last little one."

She continued down one wall, then moved to the other. She hadn't stopped crying. The room was full of children. Every shackle had been taken, except for the one that must have held the poor girl Brian had taken out, Sarah.

The first girl had come to screaming. Loralye tried to comfort her, but the girl was inconsolable. Loralye began to sing a song, all the while praying that the Lord would bring His peace to the room that had been used for far too long to bring the exact opposite.

She was surprised when the screaming stopped. As she sang, the girl began to listen to the words that Loralye belted out. Two more children still had life in them. After she got them down from the wall, they sat together, holding onto one another. Three. Out of 23 sets of chains, there were only three still alive.

She held onto the hand of the once-screaming child and continued to sing as she led the trio out of the room. Loralye was reminded of how the two disciples Paul and Silas had praised the Lord when they were once shackled in prison. The Lord had broken every chain that night with their praises, so Loralye didn't stop singing.

The girls limped along, blood speckling the floor behind them. Knowing they could leave a trail, Loralye went to the supply closet and rinsed off their legs. She then bound their wounds with the rags she had just the day before used to clean the very chains they had been shackled to moments before. She continued to sing.

After they were all cleaned up, Loralye was unsure of what to do next. She had never been anywhere beyond the rooms she and Isaiah maintained. Where should she take them? "Help me Lord," she prayed inwardly.

Deciding the only thing to do was to keep moving, Loralye took them through the door Brian always used. It was unlocked. Turning the handle, they all went inside.

"So, you are telling me you don't want to work with Loralye any longer?" Toby eyed the boy across from him suspiciously.

He normally would never have taken an audience with one so young, but his curiosity got the better of him. Toby was bewitched by Loralye, and his fascination with her followed the young man's request for a meeting.

"That's right sir. She is losing her mind, been down here too long. She's starting to say things I don't understand about a key, and someone named Carmen who was never supposed to be down here in the first place. I think she has lost it, sir."

Toby put his feet on his desk, ankles crossed. He pondered the boy's words and wondered if Loralye's cord had finally snapped. He had pushed her to limits before but was always pleasantly surprised by her strength to bounce back. Maybe he had finally broken her.

"Thank you for the information boy, I will think about it and get back with you. For now, go back to work. I will talk with her tonight and then we can meet again in the morning."

"Very good sir, thank you." With that, Isaiah left the room and began to go back upstairs, unsure what he would find.

Toby looked forward to his and Loralye's rendezvous. It had been far too long since they had spent any quality time together.

Loralye took the girls through each room as quickly as she could. The hallway was different than the ones she was used to. The rooms connected from strange angles; she was getting turned around. The key she had in her pocket had opened every door they had come to so far, and for that she was thankful.

Every time she opened another room, she prayed that no one would be on the other side. So far, the rooms had been empty. They had vials covering counters like the ones she had seen Brian with a hundred times. They were all empty.

They went through another door, another room. "Lord, you have got to get us out of here!" she prayed. The girls began to whimper again. When they turned another corner, Loralye saw a man from behind.

He turned towards her. It was Brian. The three girls all began to scream in unison and the man began to cry. "I'm not going to hurt you again, I promise."

His words did not appease them, they all cowered behind Loralye and screamed in terror. Loralye saw a stream of urine rush towards her foot. She hated that she had brought them back in front of the very man who had tortured them.

Doing her best to scream over the inconsolable girls, Loralye asked him, "How do we get out of here Brian?"

He looked at her and pushed his glasses back up his long nose. In a somber, lifeless tone, he said, "There is an elevator that way, after you get to the top floor you have to make it past several guards, I don't think you will be able to make it."

"We have to try Brian," she said.

"Of course, you do. The elevator is that way, I hope you can get out." with that, Loralye took the girls towards the elevator and prayed that God would make a way where there was no other way.

Chapter Forty

Loralye pulled the girls forward, all the while singing praises to the Lord. She knew they did not have a lot of time left. If she was going to save them, she had to move fast. When they reached the elevator, there was no button.

Loralye tried not to panic. The smallest child began to cry again, blood seeping out of the makeshift bandage Loralye had used. She knelt and pulled the cloth tighter to stop the bleeding. "It's going to be okay child, try to stay quiet." The little girl put her thumb in her mouth and did her best to quiet herself.

Focusing back on the elevator, Loralye searched for how to get the doors to open. After a few more grueling moments, she found the small key-shaped hole. Placing her key inside, she waited. They heard a motor begin. The elevator was coming.

Loralye's heart began to pound harder. She looked behind her, feeling as if they were being watched. How much time did they have left? The door opened and Loralye guided them inside, hit the number one on the button panel, shocked to see they were on floor eighteen. The machine came to life and began to pull them up.

After Isaiah walked up all the stairs to room 13, he slowly walked back down to find Porker, giving Loralye as much time as he could. When Porker was in sight, he sped up and ran to Porker after going back upstairs to find Loralye gone, following her instructions. "Porker, Porker! She's gone!"

"What do you mean she's gone? Slow down Isaiah, what are you talking about?"

"Loralye, she's gone! I told Toby something was off with her today. I went back upstairs to get back to work after meeting with him and she was not there. Room thirteen is open, all the kids are laid on the floor, off the chains. What do we do Porker?"

Porker began to panic. Taking a handkerchief out of his pocket, he dabbed at his brow. "Isaiah, there is only one thing we can do. I've gotta report it."

"Porker, it's Loralye. Isn't there something else we can do?"

"If I don't, Toby will not only deal with her but all you others too. She wouldn't want that. I'll walk slow-like and try to give her as much time as I can. God bless her, I hope she makes it out." With that, Porker headed towards Toby's office. Isaiah prayed she would make it.

The elevator took an eternity to reach the top floor. Loralye began to shake uncontrollably, the fear inside of her making itself known. She sang on, her words uneven. When they were close to the top, Loralye pulled the girls close and spoke to them in earnest.

"Girls, I know you don't know me. My name is Loralye, and I was sent to help you. We have got to be very quiet when these doors open, do you understand?"

They nodded their heads, the littlest of the group still sucking her thumb.

"Good. Now you all stay as low to the ground as you can and follow my lead. We are going to try to find the exit as quickly as possible, you understand?"

They did. They all knew this was their only chance of escape. Loralye stood back up and waited for the door to open, they were closed. The elevator dinged and the door slowly opened. Surprise almost overtook her when she saw what was on the other side.

They had been transported back into real life. Tears fell fast, Loralye swiped them away as she urged the girls to follow her. They stepped into a beautiful hallway with lush carpet that was soft under their feet.

The room was warm, a feeling Loralye hadn't known for a very long time. Thankful the hall was empty, they began to move forward, unsure of which way to go. They came to a door along the wall. Loralye put a finger to her mouth and urged them to be silent. She cracked the door open, inside was a large kitchen.

A woman was inside, kneading bread, her back to them. Loralye was unsure what to do. The decision was made for her when one of the girls sneezed and brought the woman's attention to them.

Stopping what she was doing, the woman's hand went to her mouth in surprise. "Oh, my Lord, what happened to you sweet children?" The woman took in the ratted hair, bloodied bandages, and small frames. They looked as if they had just experienced death itself. If only she knew just how true, that was.

Loralye ushered the girls in and closed the door to the hallway softly. Rushing to the woman who was still in shock, Loralye took the children to her. "I need your help. Can you get these sweet girls to safety? Will you get them out of here?"

The woman wiped her hands off on her apron, flour littering her face. "I didn't know."

"No one said you did mam, but we need your help. Will you help us? We need to go, now! We are almost out of time."

Shaken, the woman began to take off her apron. "If we go now, we can leave in the flour truck. Murphy is a friend of mine.

He will take us out of here. Come along now little ones, we must hurry."

Staring at the bread that was cooling on a rack nearby, the woman followed their gaze. Grabbing a loaf for each of them, she took her purse off a hanger on the wall and began to head towards the door that connected the kitchen to the delivery room.

Loralye walked them there, constantly looking behind her. The flour delivery van was still there, and a man was unloading the heavy sacks onto a nearby pallet. When the man saw the group come towards him, he was just as surprised as the cook.

"What's going on Martha? What happened to these girls?"

"I don't know Murphy. What I do know is we need to get them out of here, now! Will you help?"

"You know I will. You all get in the back. I can't have anyone else in front with me or they may stop me to check the van."

Murphy helped each of them into the white van. Martha got in first, then handed each girl a chunk of bread as they sat down. Loralye stood there, thankful for the sight. The girls were on their way out. They were safe. Martha urged Loralye to hurry and get in.

"I can't. I must go back and try to save my son."

An understanding passed between them. Tears slid down Martha's cheeks. "We will get them to safety, you have my word."

"Thank you." Loralye closed one of the back doors and then began to close the other. One of the girls cried out, "Wait!"

Startled at the sound, being the first Loralye had heard spoken from any of them, Loralye paused. The girl scooted to the back of the van and wrapped her arms around Loralye. Whispering, she said, "Thank you. I prayed all last night that I would get out."

Loralye held onto the girl fiercely, thankful that the Lord had chosen her to answer the girl's prayer. She let go, closed the door, and watched the van pull out of the loading dock. Loralye saw the sun glimmer on the windshield, and her skin ached to feel it, but knowing she didn't have time, Loralye rushed back the way she had come.

She retraced her steps and went back to the elevator. Placing the key inside the keyhole, she was thankful that the elevator was still on their floor. Once inside, she hit floor eighteen and waited for the metal box to take her back to her prison.

Fear gripped her, coming on hard and fast. Freedom had been at her fingertips. She could have been on her way to a normal life. But could she ever have lived a life knowing that she had left her son in the very pits of hell on earth? Loralye wouldn't have been able to, and she knew it.

Knowing the right choice had been made, she waited anxiously for the elevator door to open. When she got back down to floor 18, the floor was still empty. She ran towards the scare floor. There was no sign of Brian, and she hoped he had found a way out.

Passing the scare floor, with room thirteen's door still wide open, Loralye ran down the staircase that would take her home, take her to Brew. She ran like the wind, hoping that Isaiah had bought her enough time. She pushed the door open at the bottom of the stairs and ran right into Toby's arms.

"I thought you might come back here. It's time we had a little talk, Carmen."

Chapter Forty-One

New York, New York Present Day

Kay was proud as they walked each child up the many stairs and out to freedom. Reporters were waiting for them, the word circulating as many of the teams began to find thousands of children all over the country.

Carter held a small boy in his arms, and Kay melted as she saw him pull a sucker out of his pocket and give it to him. The boy's eyes lit up as he placed it in his mouth. His little legs began to kick as he enjoyed the sweet treat, his little feet bare in the cool fall air.

Dozens of ambulances worked their way into Central Park, as police teams took over and headed down the tunnel. Kay prayed that they would find every last child, that they would discover every tunnel.

After doing a few reports and answering a hundred questions, she, Carter, and Al worked their way through the ever-growing crowd and went back to the warehouse to check on the other teams. They watched in awe at what they saw. In the hours they had been gone, nearly every screen that had been empty when they left, now had missing children filling them.

Carol flashed between them, excited to share all that had happened with the team. They sat there for hours, watching more and more children being pulled out of the ground. Some were hurt, all were malnourished, but they were alive and for once in who knew how long, they were safe.

As the days followed, stories came flooding in. 70 percent of the locations they had staked out were entrances to the underground tunnels. Law enforcement had gotten involved in investigating the other leads they had compiled with the help of Andrea's notebook. They had arrested more than 1,000 men and saved over twenty thousand children.

Kay and Carter both were in shock over the numbers that were growing every day. They were in a stupor at the knowledge of some of the men that were involved.

Organizations that had been put in place to help children were one of the biggest culprits.

More than three-quarters of the children found were John Does. They had figured they had been born underground or brought over the border from other countries. Kay had set teams in place to try to reunite as many families as possible. It was going to take years.

Carol never did find her daughter. She did, however, find a husband. She and Al said their I do's a year later. Carter got ordained for the occasion, Hope tottled down the aisle, dumping the flower petals in a pile as soon as she set foot on the white aisle runner.

Al and Carol planned to adopt two of the children that had been brought out of hiding, the need for parents more prevalent than ever before. Carol had fallen in love with one of the little boys and they were just waiting for final approval from the home study they had done a few weeks before they got married.

Kay continued her work as Governor, her term ending soon. She had decided to take a step back from politics, the need for rest more present than ever before. She, Carter, and Hope were planning a trip to Honduras to see Paul, Jane, and Lilah. Kay couldn't wait.

A few days before they were to leave, Kay got a call from Al. He had taken a month off for an extended honeymoon and Kay couldn't be happier for them.

"Al, it is so good to hear from you! How was your trip?"

"It was good Kay, thank you again for sending us on such a lavish vacation. Carol said that she has never had so much fun."

Kay smiled. She had a lot of fun planning their trip to Europe. "Well, what can I do for you? You're not due back to work until we get back from Honduras."

"I know I know. I have a favor to ask. Do you still have that mp3? The one with Brew?"

"Of course, I do."

"I need you to bring it down to a woman in Norwalk Connecticut."

Surprised by the request, Loralye stopped what she was doing and sat down. "Al, what's going on?"

"I don't want to say."

"Can this wait until I get back?"

"Kay, I don't think it can. Trust me on this one, it will be worth your time."

Kay hung up and called her pilot. She and Carter were going to Connecticut.

The next day, Kay, Carter, and Al all boarded the private plane and took the short flight to Connecticut. She had her laptop in tow, annoyed that Al wouldn't tell her what was going on.

When the plane landed, a car picked them up and took them to a small nursing home that was just outside of town. The driver pulled up to the entrance and dropped them off.

Carter carried Kay's computer case for her, and they headed inside. Al walked them around the halls, and Kay was surprised at his familiarity with the place.

"Have you been here before Al?"

"Let's just say that Carol and I made a little pit stop on the way home. I couldn't bring you here unless, I was sure."

"Sure, of what?" Kay asked as Al stopped in front of a room.

Al smiled, then walked inside. Kay followed as he said, "Loralye, it's so good to see you again."

Kay hit stop on the mp3, the frail woman leaning back in her recliner with tears in her eyes. Her skin was paper thin, her body frail. She took another tissue from the box that sat in her lap.

"That was my boy? That was Brew?"

Kay leaned in, the love in the woman's eyes heartbreaking.

"He was an amazing man, Loralye. He saved my life more than once."

"I always knew he would be a protector. I'm so proud of him." She dabbed at her eyes, and Kay wondered how many tears the woman had cried for her son.

"Toby never would tell me what happened to him or the others. He liked to hold that over me. All the years he was around I was chained to the walls of one of the rooms somewhere in the tunnels. I begged him to let me see Brew one more time, he never would give in."

"What happened that day you saved the girls? That was the last Brew knew of you on the recording."

Loralye took a breath, then in a broken voice that only can come with age, she told her story.

"Toby was awfully mad when he got to me that day. He took me to his office. Brian was there, tied up."

"We felt a large shake all the way down there. Toby told me later they had to blow up the location I had taken the girls through. They were not able to find the driver and cook praise God. I was never told what happened to Brian, but I know he never left that place.

"I was never allowed to see Porker or the children again. Toby and one other man were the only two I saw for years. One day, Toby left and never came back. Rumors went around that he had died in a car crash, but I will never know for sure. I cannot say that I missed him."

"What happened to you after that?"

"The man who took over for Toby took a liking to me. He ended up becoming a good friend of mine. He tried to find Brew for me, but by that time Brew had been moved somewhere else. They kept things separate down there. They thought it better that way.

"If they didn't know what was going on, they couldn't give too much information out if they got caught. You would not believe all the secrets that went on down there. It was a nation all on its own.

"I spent the last thirty or forty years working in the filing system. Until my arthritis got too bad to maneuver. My friend, Charles, passed away maybe five years ago from a heart attack. He had made provisions for me to be well cared for in case anything happened to him. I was bedridden for the past few years. That is where your men found me last year. They brought me here and I've been here ever since."

"Some of the nurses around here have been kind enough to look things up for me. When they read your article in Time Magazine a few months ago, one of them reached out to try and get ahold of you. Last week, we finally heard back from Al."

"I got here just as soon as I could Loralye."

"I know you did, and I think you for that. Kay, I need to thank you too. You did what I couldn't do, you saved the children for me. For years I have prayed and prayed that God would send a Moses to those poor sweet souls, and He finally answered my prayers."

"It's you who I need to thank Loralye, not the other way around."

"What on earth could you need to thank me for?"

"You raised one of the best men I have ever known. Even though it was only for a few short years. When he found the Lord, it was as if all the teaching you had done took root and shot up in a flash. He would have adored you Loralye, he was a wonderful man."

"Thank you for telling me that. As a mother, you never feel as if you have done enough, haven't trained them well enough for the battles that are to come. Praise God that when Brew grew old, he did not depart."

"Amen to that," Carter said.

They spent the day listening to Brew's story, Loralye asking Kay to pause it several times to add to the tale that was being told. They laughed and cried together. The remembrance of old times brought both joy and sorrow.

Kay promised to return after their trip. She left the mp3 with Loralye so she could listen to her son's deep baritone voice which Loralye had said was identical to her husband Abe's.

As they walked back out to the car and headed towards the airport, Carter put his arm around Kay's shoulder and pulled her to him. "What are you thinking about babe," he asked.

"I'm thinking that a large part of my life has come to a close."

He smiled, kissed the top of her head, and said, "That's funny, I was just thinking that things were just beginning."

About The Author

Samara Risner lives on five acres in a small town in Ohio with her husband Judah and seven children Lilah, Sawyer, Loralye, Lailey, Wyley, Rhettington and Lynnah. Her love for Jesus, coffee, music and doodles keeps her busy as she homeschools, writes and serves at a local church in the same town that she grew up in.

www.ingramcontent.com/pod-product-compliance
Lightning Source LLC
Chambersburg PA
CBHW020316200626
46814CB00006BA/2264

* 9 7 8 1 7 3 7 8 9 7 4 4 6 *